T0209775

My Favorite
Words

Also by Dennis Ford

Fiction

Red Star
Landsman
Things Don't Add Up
The Watchman

Humor / Belles Lettres

Miles of Thoughts
Thinking About Everything

Psychology

Lectures on Theories of Learning
Lectures on General Psychology ~ Volume One
Lectures on General Psychology ~ Volume Two

Genealogy

Eight Generations
Genealogical Jaunts
Genealogical Musings
Genealogical Troves ~ Volume One

My Favorite
Words

Dennis Ford

MY FAVORITE WORDS

iUniverse books may be ordered through booksellers or by contacting:

iUniverse
1663 Liberty Drive
Bloomington, IN 47403
www.iuniverse.com
1-800-Authors (1-800-288-4677)

ISBN: 978-1-6632-0244-4 (sc)
ISBN: 978-1-6632-0249-9 (e)

Print information available on the last page.

iUniverse rev. date: 06/02/2020

To logophiles, everywhere

Contents

Preface

"In the beginning was the Word." That's how the *Gospel of John* opens. The word is the start for religious people. Whatever their faith, the word is the start for writers. Later on, come sentences and paragraphs and chapters and stories, but in the beginning there is the word.

For the past few years, I've kept a list of words I liked. Some words I've used. Some words I intend to use in the future—I'm hoping the opportunities will present themselves. To keep a list of words is to create a dictionary. At first, I kept this list to myself. Lately, I felt the urge to share the list. Other writers may find the list helpful in constructing their worlds of words.

There are no off-color or profane words in *My Favorite Words*. Such words can be found in dictionaries stocked behind the cash wraps in less-than-reputable bookstores. And there are no unusual words that appear strange to the eyes and foreign to the ears. Such words rarely appear in print other than in compendiums of unpronounceable words. (I included at the end of the book a list of fancy words that, although not particularly odd-looking, are best to avoid.) None of the definitions in *My Favorite Words* are intentionally clever or witty. It's not possible to compete with Ambrose Bierce's *The Devil's Dictionary*. Of course, I take full responsibility for any unclear or idiosyncratic definitions—I have to, since there's no one else to blame.

There are words to live by—we find these words in the *Gospel of John*. There are words to write with—we find a sample of these words in *My Favorite Words*. I like to think that the words in this dictionary are useful and upright, interesting and wholesome, needful and necessary, the kind of workaday words any writer would be proud to put in a sentence.

Note: words that do not appear in the English portion of *Webster's Ninth New College Dictionary* (1988) are in italics. The covers have fallen apart from use, but this book still serves as the dictionary behind my dictionary.

Word ~ the basic unit of a spoken and written language; a sound of speech that cannot be further reduced and expresses a consensually understood meaning; the written form of the spoken unit of speech.

My Favorite Nouns, Verbs and Adjectives

A

abashed ~ ashamed, embarrassed, shy

abrade, to ~ to scrape, to scrape away; to erode

abstemious ~ a person who eats and drinks sparingly

abysm ~ an abyss

adept ~ an expert in a field; in occult circles, an "ascended master"

adroit ~ successful in handling difficult situations

adventitious ~ arising from an independent, collateral source

affable ~ having a friendly, agreeable nature; an extravert

affined ~ related; having mutual obligations

affirm, to ~ to assert; to validate a belief or conclusion

afterglow ~ a glow that remains after the main light has
        extinguished

afterling ~ a subaltern, an underling

agitatione ~ bogus Latin for a state of great agitation or annoyance

a-go-go ~ a common suffix, such as whiskey-a-go-go or pizza-a-go-go
        (not to be confused with a go-go bar)

air hostess ~ a 1930s term for a flight attendant; a stewardess

alcove ~ a nook; a recessed space in a room

amaranth ~ a flower whose bloom never fades

ambiguate, to ~ to confuse a situation; to make ambiguous

amen corner ~ the corner seat in a tavern; a reserved pew in a church

anacoluthon ~ a shift of meaning in a sentence, indicated by use of a dash in writing

annulated ~ rings in an object, such as in a tree

anomalist ~ a person who studies paranormal activities; formerly a "Fortean"

aphorism ~ an apothegm, axiom, bromide, byword, chestnut, maxim, moralism precept, proverb, saw, saying, sutra, tenet

appointed ~ comfortably furnished, such as an apartment; good-looking

arch- ~ a prefix indicating prototypical or supreme, such as arch-fiend or arch-villain

arctics ~ winter clothing

ardent spirits ~ alcoholic beverages

argot ~ jargon peculiar to a particular group, such as servers in a restaurant

arm, on the ~ to buy an object on credit

arrest, to ~ to bust, to collar, to nab, to pinch, to round up, to take into custody arroyo ~ a water-carved gully; a source of water in a desert

arterioneurosis ~ a phobia about imaginary vascular diseases

ascribe, to ~ to attribute a cause for an action or belief; to hold
particular beliefs

aspergillum ~ the perforated container used to sprinkle holy water
on congregants

assent, to ~ to agree; to approve

asseverate, to ~ to state categorically and with emphasis

atavism ~ a return to a primitive time or condition

auroral ~ of the dawn

austral ~ in a southern direction

averments ~ statements declared to be true

B

babysit, to ~ to watch a person, usually a baby; standardly used
    without "for"

backlight, to ~ to light from behind or below

baffle, to ~ to confuse or bewilder, as in W.C. Fields's classic line,
    "It baffles science."

ballyhoo ~ extravagant claims about events or objects; flamboyant
    advertising

baneful ~ a dangerous substance or event, often with preternatural
    connotations

banter, to ~ to engage in light, but witty, conversation

bar ~ a tavern, saloon, barrelhouse, bucket shop, joint, tap house,
    speakeasy, canteen (American Southwest), shebeen (Irish)

barboni ~ Italian for vagrants or vagabonds

barghest ~ a demon in the shape of a dog; a hellhound

barkeep(er) ~ a bartender

baseborn ~ a person born poor; born in the lower classes

batrachian ~ like an amphibian

battlements ~ open spaces in the wall of a fort or castle

beanling ~ a small or insignificant person

beckon, to ~ to summon; something that awaits, such as eternity bedbug ~ slang for an odd character or a mentally disturbed person

bedizened ~ dressed in a gaudy or extravagant manner

bedlamite ~ a mentally disturbed person; derives from the infamous English hospital

beetle, to ~ for one object to overhang or project over another object

befool, to ~ to deceive or delude a person; to make a fool of another person

befuddled ~ bewildered, confused, perplexed

belie, to ~ to show to be false; an action or statement that shows another action or statement to be untrue

bell lap ~ the last lap of a race

bemused ~ bewildered, confused, perplexed

benighted ~ to exist in a confused and ignorant state; unenlightened

benignity ~ a form of address to an authority who is perceived as generous

betroth, to ~ an obsolete term for marriage

bevy ~ a group of objects or animals, especially fowl

bilk, to ~ to evade paying a debt

birder ~ a birdwatcher

blab, to ~ to blabber, to blather, to bleat, to jabber, to twaddle, to yap; to reveal a secret

blackguard ~ a criminal; a scoundrel

blacken, to ~ to make dark; to ruin a person's reputation; to slander a person

blanch, to ~ to shrink in fear; to turn white in fear; to flinch

blandishment ~ an alluring object; flattery

blatherskite ~ a talkative, foolish person

bleb ~ a bubble; a tiny object

blench, to ~ to flinch; to physically shrink in fear or surprise

blind ~ a hiding place, often used in hunting

blind pig ~ a Prohibition-era term for a speakeasy

bling ~ a current term for flashy clothing or jewelry

bloke ~ a chap, a fellow, a guy, usually English in nationality

blotch ~ a blemish; a disfiguring mark

bloviate, to ~ to speak in a pompous, self-important style

blowhard ~ a braggart; a boastful person

blown ~ blushing, usually in reference to rosy cheeks

blowzy ~ a red face; a sloppy style of fashion or behavior

bogus ~ a fake; something that is not true

bolt, to ~ to run or flee rapidly; to suddenly speed up

bombastic ~ a loud and aggressive style of speaking or writing

bone saw ~ what pathologists use on dead people

bonhomie ~ friendliness; geniality; hospitality

bonkers ~ a slang term for a crazy deed or a mentally disturbed
person

boom box ~ a handheld radio, usually large in size and played loud

boozehound ~ an alcoholic

boreal ~ in a northern direction

boss ~ a slang term for something that is first-rate

botched ~ an effort or a procedure that fails because of mistakes

botheration ~ the state of being vexed, mightily

bouffant ~ a puffed out and combed-up style of hair

brake ~ a green thicket, often located in a marsh

brandish, to ~ to swing a weapon aggressively

brandling ~ an earthworm used as bait

break night, to ~ to stay up all night; a New York City term

bridge-and-catch ~ a pedestrian walkway in a construction site
scaffolding; a sidewalk shed

bright eye, to ~ to serve as a lookout in the commission of a crime brindled ~ a black-and-white pattern; mottled

brown shoe service ~ service in naval air (vs. "black shoe" for service on a ship)

brumal ~ wintry conditions

brumous ~ misty; a wet fog

brunt ~ the main thrust of action or speech; gist; the receptacle of a blow

buccal ~ the mouth; the area of the mouth and cheeks

bucket shop ~ an unethical brokerage house; a disreputable tavern

bugbear ~ an impediment; a source of vexation

bug out, to ~ to leave a place in a hurry; to become anxious or panicky

bulbous ~ bulb shaped, like a nose

bumble, to ~ to make small mistakes

bummer ~ a situation that starts out well but turns out badly

bumptious ~ assertive behavior; a pushy or aggressive person

bungle, to ~ to make large mistakes; to blow, blunder, boggle, bollix up, botch, flub, mess up, muddle, muff, screw up

bunkie ~ a close companion; a person who shares one's apartment or bed bunko squad ~ a police unit specialized to catch thieves and confidence men

bunkum ~ a long-winded statement or speech full of nonsense; originated in Buncombe County, NC

burnish ~ polish on the surface of an object; glister

bushwa ~ nonsensical speaking; preposterous statements

bust outs ~ tight-fitting clothing

buzzwords ~ slogans, especially in politics

bycatch ~ fish or mammals caught in nets intended for a different species

C

cabeza ~ one's head (Spanish)

cache ~ a hiding place; hidden objects

cachet ~ a seal of approval

cackle, to ~ to laugh in a giddy or silly manner

cairn ~ a cone-shaped marker of stones used as a memorial

caitiff ~ a lowlife; a thug; a villain

calamity ~ a great disaster; a great tragedy; a catastrophe

caliginous ~ darkness; a dark place

callow ~ an immature person; a socially inexperienced person

calumny ~ slander; spreading false information about a person

camber, to ~ to curve inward; to arch

candent ~ white hot

cankered ~ decayed and splintered wood; a state of corruption

captious ~ a critical argument; a disingenuous argument

careen, to ~ to bounce; to move out of control at a high rate of
speed

carnelian ~ a blood red color

carouse, to ~ to drink and party over a lengthy period of time carpet knight ~ a soldier who bravely fights battles on paper

cat fight ~ a fist fight between women

catchpenny ~ cheap goods, such as are sold in thrift stores

catenate, to ~ to place items in a series; to join or link a number of items

cenotaph ~ an empty tomb for a person buried elsewhere

cerements ~ burial cloths in which only the face shows

chalk up to, to ~ to credit an outcome to a person or behavior

chanteuse ~ a female nightclub singer

chapfallen ~ to be in a depressed and melancholy mood

charisma ~ having personal charm and influence; a gift bestowed by God

charnel ~ a place where lots of deaths occurred; a place to keep corpses

chary ~ to be hesitant; to be leery

cheek, to ~ to pretend to swallow prescription medications

chelonian ~ turtle-like; having the face or shell of a turtle

cherub ~ an angel of knowledge; a beautiful child

chill box ~ the place where corpses are kept in morgues

chink ~ a nick, as in armor or metal

chintzy ~ gaudy and cheap clothes or objects

chomp on, to ~ to bite, to gnaw; to think deeply about a topic; to obsess

chortle, to ~ to laugh; a combination of a chuckle and a snort

choto ~ lamb (Spanish)

chthonic ~ a primitive condition or state

chubette ~ a full-figured woman busting out of her clothing

chuck, to ~ to throw, often in an aggressive and careless manner

chug, to ~ to move heavily in a plodding manner, like a freight train

chum ~ a close friend; chopped fish used for bait

chump ~ a person easily taken advantage of; a dupe; a mark

church key ~ a bottle opener

churlish ~ peevish; a person who is unpleasantly disagreeable

citrine ~ a yellow color

clabber ~ sour milk; curdled milk

clamber, to ~ to climb hastily and clumsily

clang ~ a hollow sound, such as one metal striking another

clash, to ~ to fight or give battle; to argue over a belief or principle clasp, to ~ to hold tightly; to grab firmly

clatter ~ noisy chatter; the banging of plates

clinch, to ~ to win; to determine an outcome; to clasp, to clench

clinquant ~ gaudy and cheap trinkets

clipper ~ an airplane (1940s term)

clock, to ~ to knock a person out with a punch; to sell drugs
        (Newark, NJ, term, 1980s)

cloying ~ behavior that is deliberately sentimental

club cat ~ a lounge lizard; a person who frequents taverns

clump ~ a group, like a clump of trees; a heavy, noisy style of
        walking

clunker ~ a beat-up old car that barely runs; a jalopy

clutch ~ an informal group, like people around the coffee machine

Coaley ~ Satan (Ozark term)

coarsen, to ~ to use uncivil speech; to engage in brutish behavior

coffee ~ crank, jo, java

coffer ~ a place, such as a safe, where valuables are stored

cognoscenti ~ people with inside knowledge; experts in a particular
        field

coiffure ~ one's hair style; hair professionally styled

collateral damage ~ civilian casualties in a military operation

compendious ~ a brief and thorough summary of a topic; a precis

confabulate, to ~ to make up events; to add details when memory fails

confluence ~ a joining of two events; a meeting of two streams

confused ~ befogged, befuddled, bemused, benumbed, nonplussed, stupefied

conk, to ~ to hit on the head; a machine that fails to operate

contemn, to ~ to despise or treat with contempt or disrespect

contrarian ~ a person who frequently argues against popular opinion

contretemps ~ an awkward event or a social mishap

contumacy ~ defiance; a refusal to comply with instructions

coop, to ~ to sleep on the job; 1960s New York term used in reference to police officers

cop, to ~ to steal; to grab; to take or obtain

cop a sneak, to ~ to leave stealthily

cordon ~ barriers with ropes, as are placed in theaters and airports

corkboard ~ a bulletin board

corner office ~ where executives work; often comes with a private toilet corona ~ a halo

corvine ~ like a crow

cosset, to ~ to pamper a person; to dandle a baby or child

costive ~ to be unresponsive; a failure to act promptly; constipated

cotton to, to ~ to exhibit a liking for a person or event

covey ~ a group of birds

crackle, to ~ to make a sizzling sound, such as fire makes

crapulent ~ being intoxicated or hung over

crassitude ~ something that is gross or coarse

cravat ~ a necktie

craven ~ cowardly; defeated

crawl, to ~ to move on one's belly, like a snake; to move slowly,
        like traffic

cream, to ~ to smash into; to beat up

credenza ~ a dresser or bureau in a bedroom

credulity ~ a naïve and gullible state; believability; a condition that
        is often strained

creen, to ~ to lean sideways (Ozark term)

creep, to ~ to move on one's hands and knees, like a reptile

creepstep, to ~ to move slowly and in an unusual manner, as on
        one's toes; often used in reference to the clergy

crenated ~ scalloped

crinkle, to ~ to wrinkle; to form in rills

crock ~ nonsense; falsehoods; also a pot

crocodilian ~ relating to crocodiles and alligators

cropper ~ a major debacle; something that causes failure

crunch, to ~ to crowd together in a small space; to bite noisily

cubby ~ a tiny pace; a cramped space

cudgel ~ a short thick stick, like a police officer's night stick

culch ~ sea shells, especially oyster shells; junk; trash

culinarian ~ a chef; a gourmand; a gourmet; a student in cooking
        school

cull, to ~ to select from a group; to reduce in number, such as a
        herd

culpable ~ to be responsible; to be blameworthy

cumber, to ~ to put obstacles in the path of travelers; to hinder
        progress

cumbersome ~ a difficult task; a large object difficult to move

cuneal ~ wedge shaped; shaped like a corner

cunning women ~ a fortune teller

curate's egg ~ a badly cooked meal that cannot be criticized

cut out ~ a CIA term for a fake identity

cynosure ~ an egotist, a narcissist; a know-it-all

D / E

damson ~ a purple or plum color

dandle, to ~ to pamper; to cosset; to hold a baby

darkled ~ a dark place; a hidden place

dashiki ~ a loose-fitting shirt worn in Africa

dawdle, to ~ to delay or dally; to waste time; to hesitate

deadfall ~ a clump of dead trees

debility ~ a disability; a physical weakness

debouch, to ~ to march an army into enemy territory

déclassé ~ to act like a member of the low class; to act in a
thuggish manner

decry, to ~ to openly oppose or condemn

deflect, to ~ to knock off course; to deviate from the correct course

defunct ~ obsolete; no longer in operation

deracinate, to ~ to pull up by the roots

detritus ~ erosion of rocks; deposits of litter left behind

devil's advocate ~ a person designated to be critical of a claim,
such as a miracle

devil's claws ~ the blades of light that dramatically shine through
cumulus clouds

diablerie ~ lore about the devil; devilish mischief; black magic

dibs on, to have ~ to stake ownership; to make claims on a place or
object

dicey ~ risky, dangerous; a treacherous situation

didactic ~ pedantic; relating to educational lessons or material

diddle, to ~ to dawdle; to manipulate with the hands in a half-
hearted manner

digs ~ one's home or apartment

dinghy ~ a small boat; a lifeboat; a rowboat

dirigible ~ a Zeppelin; a rigid airship unlike a soft-framed "blimp"

dirty, to ~ to sully or besmear

disambiguate, to ~ to clear up confusion, especially of an
intellectual nature

discombobulated ~ confused, bewildered, out-of-sorts

discotheque ~ a 1970s dance club

disdain, to ~ to express contempt of a person or principle

disincarnate ~ a ghost; a spirit

disparage, to ~ to asperse, to belittle, to defame, to malign

disparate ~ different elements or paths; various components of an
object

dispose, to ~ to decide a matter; to be inclined; to make plans; to get rid of something

disquisition ~ a learned treatise; an intellectual investigation

dissemble, to ~ to pretend not to notice; to conceal under false pretenses

dodder, to ~ to act feebly like an old person; to move shakily and unsteadily

dodge, to ~ to escape responsibility by luck or by deceit; to avoid a bad situation

dog it, to ~ to not make a complete effort; to shirk one's duty

doll up, to ~ to dress in the height of fashion to party and carouse

dollface ~ an attractive woman (Prohibition-era term)

doozy, doozer ~ an amazing event; an amazing accomplishment

dornick ~ a brick or rock, usually thrown at someone

draggy ~ to move in a slow or weak manner

dragonfly ~ damselfly, darner, darning needle, mosquito hawk, snake doctor

dragooned ~ forced to participate in an event; shanghaied

drivel ~ nonsensical speech; lips covered with slaver; slobber

drop cloth ~ a dish rag

druid ~ a Celtic priest; Celtic cognoscenti

druthers ~ one's choice; one's preference

dulcify, to ~ to make beautiful; to sweeten

dun ~ a brown or gray color

dun, to ~ to hound a person for money; to nag a person for something

dunk, to ~ to become submerged; to place an item in a liquid

dunnage ~ packing material

dupe ~ a person who does not know the true situation

dutch ~ fake, such as fake perfume; to take separate checks at a dinner

dwindle, to ~ to reduce in number or potency; to shrink

earwig, to ~ to influence a decision by a private conversation

ebullient ~ exuberant; bubbly

ecliptic ~ the path of the sun across the sky

ectoplasm ~ a substance secreted by mediums that disincarnates use to materialize

elementals ~ nature spirits; spiritual forces of nature

elsewise ~ otherwise

elude, to ~ to escape capture or discipline; to avoid a situation successfully elusive ~ something that is hard to obtain or locate; something hidden

embattled ~ being in a state of battle; being under attack for a long period

embittered ~ feeling resentment and bitterness toward others

enchant, to ~ to bewitch, often by magical means; to fascinate

enlistee ~ a man or woman who enters the armed services voluntarily

ersatz ~ an inferior substitute

erstwhile ~ former, as in friend

escritoire ~ a writing desk

estival ~ relating to summer

eurythmic ~ harmonious body movements, such as in ballet

extra man ~ a bachelor

eye black ~ eye shadow used in sports; lampblack

eye slits ~ the eyes, especially when small

F

fair-spoken ~ soft-spoken; conciliatory words

falter, to ~ to fail to accomplish a goal; to stumble

fanlight ~ a semicircular window over a door

fantasist ~ a person who engages in fantasies; an imaginative
      person

farmer ~ bumpkin, clodbuster, clodhopper, cornhusker, hayseed,
      hick, hillbilly, homesteader, rube, sodbuster; yahoo, yokel

farrago ~ a hodgepodge; a medley; a mixture of items

fastidious ~ a meticulous person who is attentive to details

fastness ~ a remote place; a wild and uninhabited place

faux ~ something that is fake or artificial

faux pas ~ a gaffe; a social blunder, contrasted with *au fait*

feather merchant ~ a coward

feckless ~ to show weakness or cowardice

fell ~ a moor; a hill (Old English)

felonious ~ behavior that constitutes a serious crime

feral ~ a wild animal; like a wild animal

ferruginous ~ rust-colored

fess up to, to ~ to admit to a mistake or a misdeed

fickle ~ erratic; unreliable; unstable

finical ~ fastidious; meticulous; given to specific preferences

firebrand ~ an agitator; a person who incites others to political
activity

first water ~ the best portion of a liquid

fishy ~ an event or action that is not authentic or meant to deceive;
dodgy

fistic ~ mean-spirited; physically tough

flabbergasted ~ a state of wonderment or amazement, often in
surprise; gobsmacked

flagitious ~ excessively wicked; blatantly evil

flapdoodle ~ a contentious argument over a trivial topic

flapper ~ a female version of the male "lounge lizard" (1920s term)

flatline, to ~ to die

flecked ~ spotted; streaked

flimsical ~ frivolous; lightweight; shoddily constructed

flinch, to ~ to duck out of the way; to recoil; to wince; to blench

flinty ~ fistic; hard-hearted; stern and mean-spirited

flippant ~ an offhanded remark that does not take a situation
seriously

flirt, to ~ to talk or behave in a manner intended to promote
        romance

flobbage ~ debris; sea shells that collect on a beach

florescent ~ blossoming; flourishing

flummery ~ nonsense; false flattery; a pretense

flummox, to ~ to deliberately confuse a person; to pretend to
        flatter a person

flunky ~ a lackey; a go-fer; a servant

flyblown ~ impure; soiled; contaminated

flyspeck ~ a detailed analysis of a topic; a tiny object

folly ~ a building or an endeavor misguided in conception

footless ~ a foolish or inept person or deed; having no support

forehanded ~ prudent; thoughtful; showing foresight

forestall, to ~ to prevent something from happening

forfend, to ~ to prevent or forbid an action

fracas ~ a fight

fraid cellar ~ a cellar in the Midwest in which to stay safe during
        storms

fram ~ raspberry red in color

freak ~ an aficionado, such as a speed freak or exercise freak friable ~ easily crumpled; brittle

frigelid ~ very cold and very hard

frippery ~ something that is extravagant and unnecessary

frisson ~ an exciting event; a state of excitement

frost, to ~ to shun or ignore a person

frowsy ~ a disheveled appearance; a stale odor

fuddy-dud ~ a spoilsport; a person reluctant to take a challenge; an old foggy

fuliginous ~ smoky light, such as caused by fire or fog

funskate ~ a person is lively and exciting to be around; a live wire

fustian ~ pretentious talk or prose

fusty ~ malodorous; moldy; old-fashioned

G

gab, to ~ to chatter; to talk incessantly about minor matters; to gossip

gabble, to ~ to talk rapidly; to gab; to jabber; to babble

gabfest ~ an informal and extended conversation involving a number of people

gad about, to ~ to stroll about aimlessly; to moon about; to swan around

gainsay, to ~ to contradict a statement; to argue against a specific point

gallant ~ a person or action judged to be honest, considerate, or noble

gallimaufry ~ a hodgepodge; a gumbo; a mixture of many items

gallop, to ~ to run at maximum speed

galumph, to ~ to walk heavily or awkwardly; to stagger

gammon ~ bacon; ham; deceptive conversation

garble, to ~ to confuse an argument; to speak in an incoherent manner

garrulity ~ talkativeness; disorganized and rambling speech

gavone ~ a glutton; a person with poor manners (Italian)

gestatorial chair ~ what the pope used to be carried on

gesticulate, to ~ to move one's hands in coordination with speaking

gibber, to ~ to talk in an incomprehensible manner; to talk gibberish

gibbous ~ something that protrudes; the moon at three quarters full

gimcrack ~ a cheap item that looks expensive

girlie bar ~ a bar that features strippers; a go-go bar

gist ~ the main point of a story or argument, often simplified; brunt

glad hand, to ~ to extend an offer to assist

glassine ~ clear plastic bag used for chocolates or for drugs

glimmers ~ the headlights of a car

glitter people ~ trend setters; wealthy party types who live dissolute lives

glob ~ a round mass; a blob

glom, to ~ to steal something; to cop; to take everything available; to eat rapidly

glop ~ a mass of unpleasant substances

gloss, to ~ to conceal or downplay something by misspeaking

gnaw, to ~ to bite, to chew; to obsess on a topic; to experience a persistent feeling

gnomic ~ a cryptic saying

gorbelly ~ an overweight person; possessing a large belly

grandee ~ a rich and important person

grapple, to ~ to wrestle; to study or debate serious issues

grasp, to ~ to clutch, to hold; to understand a concept

gravid ~ pregnant

great house ~ a mansion

greensward ~ a well-watered green lawn

grifter ~ a con man, especially one who travels extensively

grindhouse ~ an old movie theater; theaters that played second-rate
    movies

grisly ~ a gory scene or place, usually involving crimes or horror

grit ~ courage and determination; pluck; sand or specks

grizzled ~ gray and wrinkled; unshaven, usually in reference to
    elderly men

grouse, to ~ to complain; to grumble; to be grumpy

growler ~ a paper or plastic container into which beer was poured

grub ~ larva; a sexless or immature creature

grungy ~ a dirty place; an unclean person

grunt ~ an enlisted soldier (Vietnam era term)

guido ~ slang for a young Italian man; a stereotype of someone
    excessively masculine

gulch ~ a deep drop in a stream, such as the kind Oliver Hardy
   used to step into

gulp, to ~ to drink rapidly; to swallow noisily

gumbo ~ a hodgepodge; a medley of disparate items; a stew (New
   Orleans)

gun for, to ~ to take aim at a person in order to defeat or ruin the
   person

gunslinger ~ Hollywood term for an Old West "shootist"

gussy up, to ~ to dress fancily

gutsy ~ a behavior or a decision that shows courage or audacity;
   grit; pluck

H

habiliments ~ clothing used in a profession; uniforms

hachure ~ shading in artwork; shadowy lines on a bright surface

haggard ~ a sickly appearance; a rundown and gaunt appearance

Hail Mary ~ a desperation pass in football; an improbable attempt

halidom ~ a repository for relics; a sacred place

handgun ~ chopper, heater, piece, rod, roscoe

handle ~ a name on the internet or short-wave radio; an alias

hanker for, to ~ a strong desire for something; a yearning

haptic ~ pertaining to the sense of touch

harangue, to ~ to use loud aggressive speech; to criticize loudly

hard by ~ close by, nearby

hard down ~ hard liquor; an unadulterated beverage

hard on for ~ a desire to get something; a hankering; a yearning

harrow, to ~ a dangerous adventure; to cut holes in the ground

harum-scarum ~ crazy disorganized behavior

hash of ~ a gumbo; a hodgepodge of disparate items

haute ~ upper-class individuals; cultured people

haute cuisine ~ what the haute eat

hauteur ~ arrogance; a know-it-all attitude

heartthrob ~ a handsome man

heel ~ a villain; a toady or unctuous person; a despicable person

heft, to ~ to lift something heavy

hell pups, hellions ~ rough young boys or men performing mischief

hell spawn ~ born of hell, such as demons or evil humans

hemal ~ the color of blood; relating to blood

heme ~ an iron substance found in meat and in many natural items; a reddish color

hepatic ~ liver-colored; relating to the liver

Herculean ~ a task requiring extraordinary effort; having great strength

hew, to ~ to cut or chop up; to hack at something

hidebound ~ a person who is very conservative; a traditionalist

hiemal ~ relating to winter; hibernal

high five ~ a greeting or sign of congratulation made by slapping palms

high-muck-a-muck ~ an arrogant person in a position of authority

hitch in ~ time spent in a place, such as in the service or in a prison hoistway ~ an elevator shaft

hokey ~ something that is obviously phony or contrived

hokum ~ bunkum; pretentious or deceptive speech

homeboys ~ friends; members of one's gang

homiletics ~ preaching; sermonizing

hone for, to ~ a desire for; a hankering (Ozark)

hoodwink, to ~ to deceive or cheat a person

Hooverville ~ a shanty town inhabited by homeless people
(Depression-era term)

hornswoggle, to ~ to bamboozle a person; to commit a hoax

house man ~ a janitor; a hotel worker

hull, to ~ to shuck; to remove a shell; to remove a covering

hunker down, to ~ to crouch; to resist altering one's position; to
double down

hustings ~ a stand on which politicians make speeches

hyacinthine ~ a purplish color

I / J

iatrogenic ~ an illness produced by the treatment of another illness

icefall ~ a frozen waterfall

ichor ~ what flows in the arteries of Greek gods and goddesses

ignominy ~ a state of embarrassment or shame

illimitable ~ endless; immeasurable; without bounds

ill-boding ~ a portent that signifies something bad is about to occur

ill-sorted ~ poorly matched or organized items

imaginable ~ something that can be imagined; something that can
be accomplished

immingled ~ mixed thoroughly; combined

impassion, to ~ to become excited or enthused about a person or
item

impassive ~ unemotional; lacking feelings

imperil, to ~ to endanger

implacable ~ a person who will not change his or her opinion

importunate ~ persistent behavior; pestering

improbable ~ an event that is unlikely to occur; a condition
unlikely to happen

impugn, to ~ to assail by argument; to challenge an argument or a
 reputation

inamorata ~ a sweetheart; a female lover

inanity ~ a pointless or foolish event or behavior

incunabulum ~ an original copy of a text; a very old text

indefatigable ~ untiring; never stopping

indemnify, to ~ to secure against loss

indulgent ~ a lenient person or policy that gives free reign to
 behavior

ineffable ~ something that is so great it cannot be described

ineludible, ineluctable ~ a fate or outcome that cannot be avoided

inextricable ~ a problem that is insoluble; a situation that cannot be
 improved

inimical ~ something that opposes or challenges a viewpoint or
 practice

insouciant ~ nonchalant; a carefree attitude

inured ~ used to pain or discomfit; acceptance of one's situation

invidious ~ something that causes harm in a slow and subtle
 manner

irascible ~ a person who has a bad temper or who is constantly
 angry

irenic ~ peaceful

iridescence ~ glistening, rainbow-like colors

iridic ~ pertaining to the iris of the eye

-ista ~ placed at the end of a word to indicate a stereotype, like
tourista

jail ~ can, gray-bar hotel, hoosegow, joint, pokey, slammer

jakes ~ a toilet, an outhouse, a privy, a water closet

jalopy ~ an old car that still runs; a junker

japery ~ disparagement expressed in an offhanded or joking
manner

jellyass ~ a coward

Jesuitical ~ a scholarly argument; an argument made using
minutiae

jim-dandy ~ to feel swell; to feel great

jimjams ~ a Civil War term for intoxication or delirium tremens

jitney ~ a small bus

jitter, to ~ to move nervously; to move repetitively; to be anxious

joggle, to ~ to walk with a bouncing gait

johnboat ~ a flat boat maneuvered in inland rivers with a pole

jolt, to ~ to suffer a sudden reverse; to be shocked or greatly
surprised

jot ~ a small mark

jotter ~ a small book used for keeping notes

jounce, to ~ to bounce; to move up and down

judder, to ~ to shake or rattle

jugglery ~ a deception; trickery

juju ~ an object of fetish

jumble, to ~ to create a hodgepodge; to confuse the order of a
        series

juncture ~ occurring at a point of time; a geographical intersection

K

kabob ~ small cubes of meat and vegetables served on a skewer

kaddish ~ the funeral prayers in Judaism

kalpa ~ an immense period of time (Hindu term)

kaput ~ something that is finished; something that is out of order

katzenjammer ~ a noisy and confused state, usually made by
children; a ruckus

keck, to ~ to retch

keen, to ~ to lament; to utter a cry for the dead

keep ~ a castle or fortress

keepsake ~ a treasured memento

kelpie ~ a malevolent spirit that causes sailors to drown (Scottish
term)

kempt ~ a well-kept place, such as a trimmed lawn

ken ~ the range of vision; how far one can see

kendo ~ fencing with bamboo poles (Japanese term)

kenspeckled ~ something that is conspicuous or obvious

kepi ~ a Civil War cap

kersey ~ woolen work clothes

key club ~ a private club

keyhole ~ an opportunity to spy on a person

kibosh, to ~ to put a stop to something

kick off, to ~ to commence; the start of a football game

kilter, out of ~ out of working order

-kin ~ a suffix meaning small, as in babykin

kinesthesia ~ sensations arising from the movements of muscles

kingfish ~ the boss; the kingpin

king-size ~ larger than standard size

kink ~ an odd quality; a characteristic that causes trouble

kiosk ~ a small structure for selling newspapers or retail items

kishka ~ blood sausage (Polish term)

kit ~ a small bag holding various items, like a shaving kit

kite, to ~ to cash checks fraudulently

kith ~ friends and distant relatives

kittenish ~ cloying and affectionate behavior

klavern ~ a local branch of the Ku Klux Klan

kneehole ~ the space under a desk for the legs

knell, to ~ the sound of bells announcing a death; to foretell failure or disaster

knobby ~ having small knobs like a tree

knock, to ~ to find fault with; to criticize; to strike

knockabout ~ an object that is sturdy and durable

knock off; to ~ to kill; to defeat; to stop work; to complete a task; to deduct a small amount of money; to produce an inferior copy

knock over, to ~ to rob a bank

knurl ~ a small knob; a serrated object that can be gripped

kolo ~ a Slavic dance in which people form a circle and jump up and down on bended knees

kook ~ an oddball; a mentally disturbed person

kowtow, to ~ to bow and grovel; to obey

K-ration ~ packaged food for soldiers in World War Two

kudo, kudos ~ praise or compliments

kumquat ~ a citrus fruit made famous by W.C. Fields

L

labile ~ changeable; unstable

labyrinthine ~ like a labyrinth or maze; a complex or obtuse topic

lace, to ~ to tie or join together; to pass through an eyelet; to spice liquor

lackey ~ a flunky; a go-fer; a yes-man

laconic ~ terse; spoken or written exactly to the point

lacteal ~ milk-like

lacuna ~ a missing part; empty or blank space between items

lacustrine ~ relating to lakes

laggard ~ a person who moves more slowly than others; a lazy person

laguna ~ a pond, lake or inlet not connected to a larger body of water

lam, on the ~ to be hiding from law enforcement

lambast, to ~ to attack verbally; to criticize aggressively

lambent ~ a flickering or shining light; a reflection of light off a surface

lamebrained ~ a misconceived project or scheme that is bound to fail

lamia ~ a female vampire or demon

lamp, to ~ to look intensely at a person, often used lasciviously

land poor ~ owning land, but having insufficient funds to
 develop it

languid ~ sluggish; weak

languish, to ~ to become weak or depressed; to suffer pain and
 negative emotions

languor ~ weariness or sluggishness brought on by the climate or
 by romance

lanuginous ~ downy; covered with soft hair

large-hearted ~ generous

larine ~ relating to sea gulls; the sound of the laughter of gulls

lascivious ~ filled with sexual cravings

lassitude ~ fatigue; boredom; listlessness

laudanum ~ a tincture of opium formerly used by physicians

layabout ~ a lazy person, frequently unemployed

lazy tongs ~ an instrument elderly or crippled people use to
 retrieve items

leastways, leastwise ~ at least

leather, to ~ to thrash, to beat with a strap

leatherneck ~ a Marine (World War One term)

lech, to ~ to lust after; to lamp

DENNIS FORD

lechery ~ insatiable interest in things sexual

legend ~ a cover story used by the CIA for an agent; a false identity

legerity ~ quickness of mind; a demonstration of wit or cleverness

leggy ~ having long or shapely legs; said of a woman

leitmotif ~ a recurring theme or melody

lemma ~ a side explanation for an unknown word or complex
         theme

lemures ~ spirits of the dead in the Roman religion (Latin term)

lengthways, lengthwise ~ in a longitudinal direction

lentic ~ living in ponds or still water; limnetic

letch ~ sexual desires and cravings; lechery

licentious ~ obviously sexual behavior and motives; immoral
            behavior

lickerish ~ something that is tempting, often used in a sexual way

lickspittle ~ an obsequious person; a sycophant; a toady

lift, to ~ to steal; to revoke a decision or proscription

lillipin ~ a short person

liminal ~ above the visual threshold; contrasted with subliminal

limpid ~ perfectly clear, such as an image or a text

lionize, to ~ to hold a person in great regard; to adulate

literati ~ a member of the intelligentsia

living water ~ flowing water

loll, to ~ to be idle; to pass the time idly; to be in a relaxed posture

long pig ~ Polynesian term for human flesh, frequently provided by missionaries

looking glass ~ a mirror

loophole ~ an escape clause in a contract; a way to break a contract

lopsided ~ leaning to one side; crooked; one-sided result in sports

lovelorn ~ having no lover; devoid of love

lovesome ~ lovely; attractive; worthy of love

lucid ~ clear, limpid, transparent; being sane and clear-minded

luciferous ~ bringing light; causing intellectual illumination

lugubrious ~ exaggerated sadness or depression

luke-hearted ~ lacking affection or motivation; a half-hearted effort

lumpen class ~ the lowest class in Marxist theory; unemployed people; the baseborn

lunette ~ crescent shaped

lurch, to ~ to stumble; to move forward in a clumsy manner

lustrous ~ luminous; bright; transparent

M

machismo ~ male bravado and preening; used in a stereotypical and derogatory manner

mackled ~ blurred; a double impression in printing or photography

maelstrom ~ raging waters; a whirlpool

magnamin ~ the maximum minimum

magnific ~ extravagant; pompous

magpie ~ a bird who collects items indiscriminately

maim, to ~ to injure in such a way as to cause permanent disfigurement or disability

malarkey ~ a statement that is obviously false; nonsense

malediction ~ to utter a curse directed at a person; to speak badly of a person

malefic ~ evil; hateful

malign, to ~ to besmirch; to speak badly of another; to slander a person

malocchio ~ the evil eye (Italian term); a belief we can curse people by staring at them

malodorous ~ to smell badly

mammalogy ~ the scientific study of mammals

mangi, to ~ to eat (Italian term)

maniacal ~ evil; sinister; deliberately vicious

manqué ~ a failure at a chosen profession; used after the name of the profession

mantled ~ a blushed or flushed look; something that is hidden

mantra ~ a mystical word or phrase (Hindu term); a phrase repeated over and over

marbled ~ well-shaped; an object that is sharply cut

marge ~ the edge of a geographical feature, such as a riverbank

marplot ~ a person who spoils or ruins things

marrow ~ the pith, as of a bone or a tree; the inside of an object

materialize, to ~ to appear suddenly, usually said of ghosts or spirits

matutinal ~ early in the morning; the morning hours

maul, to ~ to attack savagely; to defeat thoroughly

mawkish ~ overly sentimental style of writing or speaking; sappy; spoony

mazy ~ resembling a maze; a confused or complicated topic

mealy-mouthed ~ cowardly speech that is deceptive or duplicitous

meegens ~ a queasy state brought on by excessive use of alcohol

mercurial ~ a changeable disposition; an impulsive person

meretricious ~ pretentious; misleadingly desirable

métier ~ to perform work for which one is prepared; a career or vocation

mewl, to ~ to make whimpering sounds

miasma ~ vapors that cause sickness; fog

middling ~ a state of moderation, usually used in the phrase "fair to middling"

mien ~ one's appearance or style of behavior; one's disposition

miffed ~ angry, usually because of a person or event that does not occur as expected

mill, to ~ to swirl; to thrash

milquetoast ~ a timid or cowardly person

mince, to ~ to cut up; to restrain speech; to withhold one's opinions

minutiae ~ trivial details that, when attended to, overwhelm a person

moil, to ~ to churn, such as water; to make dirty; to toil at boring work

molder, to ~ to rot; to disintegrate

moll ~ the wife or girlfriend of a criminal

molt, to ~ to lose feathers or shed skin

mooch, to ~ to take something with no expectation of paying it back

moolah ~ slang for money

moon, to ~ to show one's derriere; to wander aimlessly; to daydream

mooncusser ~ a Colonial-era bandit in Southern New Jersey

moop ~ a lazy or dumb person; a member of the lumpen class

mordant ~ sarcastic in speech or writing

morello ~ a dark red color; a cherry color

mortmain ~ the influence of the past on the present; inherited wealth or property

mossback ~ an old-fashioned person who refuses to change with the times

mote ~ a tiny object; a speck

mottled ~ a spotted or speckled surface

mouthy ~ a talkative person

mucilaginous ~ a substance that is thick and sticky, like gum

muckrake, to ~ to search for scandals, especially among prominent people

mucoid ~ moldy; resembling mucus

muddle through, to ~ to succeed despite making errors; to barely succeed

mudra ~ religious hand and finger gestures (Hindu term)

muffle, to ~ to stifle; to suppress or restrain; to mute sounds mufti ~ civilian clothes worn by members of the armed services

muliebrity ~ feminine softness; the opposite of masculine virility

mulish ~ obstinate behavior; a refusal to budge

mull, to ~ to ponder; to think something over before acting

mulligan ~ a second chance; a free shot in golf

murine ~ rat-like; rodent-like

muss, to ~ to mess up, especially the hair; to disarrange

mutt ~ slang for a lowlife or unattractive male

N / O

nail, to ~ to hit; to nab or catch; to be on target

nary ~ an obsolete term for "not one"

nascent ~ a newborn; something that recently came into existence

nebulous ~ misty; brumous; an unclear or vague statement

nepenthe ~ a substance that makes one forget

Neronian ~ an extravagant person, place or party

nervy ~ audacity, boldness, courage

nethermost ~ the lowest geographical point

New York minute ~ hectic events that occur in a short period of
time

nib ~ a small protruding or projecting part

nibble on, to ~ to eat sparingly or slowly

nibs, his or her ~ slang for an important person or authority figure

niccolite ~ a pale red color

niggard ~ a miser; a stingy person

niggle, to ~ to become preoccupied with minutiae

night soil ~ human fertilizer

-nik ~ a suffix used to describe a type of person, such as peacenik nilpotent ~ having no effect; zero effect

nimp ~ a nincompoop; a foolish or ignorant person

nitwit ~ a foolish or ignorant person

nocturnal ~ referring to the night; occurring at night

noisome ~ malodorous; noxious

nonplussed ~ bewildered; stupefied; at a sudden loss for words

no-see-em ~ biting insects that are not visible

nub ~ the gist of something

nudge ~ a person who nags another person into doing something

nudge, to ~ to try to influence a person; to coerce a person into
    action

numinous ~ a spiritual, often preternatural, place or experience

obeisance ~ deference to an authority figure

obfuscate, to ~ to confuse; to cloud an issue; to darken

oblation ~ an offering or gift in a religious service

obliquity ~ a confused statement; an immoral thought or deed

obsequious ~ excessively subservient; excessively obedient
    behavior

obtrude, to ~ to intrude in a harsh or impolite way

occultation ~ a disappearance of a person or object, as if by magic occultist ~ a person interested in paranormal topics; an anomalist

oddball ~ a strange or eccentric person; a person who does not
conform

off-brand ~ a cheap bottle of liquor or perfume; bottom-shelf liquor

ogham ~ an ancient style of writing in Ireland using straight lines
and notches

oilcloth ~ a waterproof rag

-ola ~ a suffix describing a condition (sickola) or behavior (payola)

oleaginous ~ oily; unctuous

oncoming ~ an event that will occur in the future

oneiric ~ pertaining to dreams

opaque ~ difficult to comprehend; not transparent

ophidian ~ like a snake or a serpent

-oso ~ a suffix describing a type of person (Mafioso)

other place, the ~ the afterlife

oust, to ~ to remove a person from power

P / Q

paggle, to ~ to hang loosely

palimpsest ~ an older text that is visible beneath a more recent text

palooka ~ a dumb muscular man

Palookaville ~ the place where dumb muscular men live

palpation ~ a doctor's touch during a physical examination

pamper, to ~ to coddle; to cosset

pannier ~ a basket on a bicycle

Parliament whiskey ~ legally sold liquor, compared to illegal
moonshine

paroxysm ~ a sudden excited or emotional state; a fit

pastoral ~ rural; rustic; sermons or actions by a pastor of a church

patter, to ~ to make small talk; to talk very rapidly

pavid ~ shy; timid

pavonine ~ like a peacock; dressed in a flashy style

peach, to ~ to inform on; to squeal

peachblown ~ blushing; a rosy complexion

peachy ~ something that is desirable or agreeable

pearlescent ~ to shine like a pearl

peel, to ~ to strip; to remove a cover

peen ~ the prongs of a fork or hammer

peep, to ~ to look at events one is not supposed to see; to chirp like a bird

pellucid ~ perfectly clear and understandable

pensile ~ hanging, such as a pendant or earrings

pepper, to ~ to pester; to shoot at; to present things or words quickly

percolate, to ~ to diffuse through a permeable substance, like coffee grinds

pergola ~ a lattice on which plants grow; a trellis

persiflage ~ banter; idle talk; patter

piddling ~ a small amount

piebald ~ composed of different elements; a black and white pattern

Pile, The ~ the on-site debris of the World Trade Center after the 9-11 attacks

pinky square ~ to make a honest statement or deal (New York slang)

piquant ~ charming; acceptably provocative; spicy

pirate ~ a freebooter, a privateer

piscine ~ like a fish

piss ant ~ an insignificant person

piss poor ~ dirt poor

pittance ~ a small amount, usually used in reference to money

platitude ~ a banal or trite saying

player ~ a person who is influential and who associates with other
influential people

plop, to ~ to sit or fall down; to thump; to thwack; to make a
thudding sound

plug away at, to ~ to shoot at; to work diligently at a task

plummy ~ something that is attractive or desirable; peachy

plump ~ overweight; a full-figured person; pursy

plutonian ~ relating to the underworld; hell

pluvial ~ rainy weather

pokey ~ slang for a jail; a small place in which to stay or live

ponderable ~ a possibility worthy of consideration

pongid ~ like an ape

poop-noddy ~ a fool (Old English)

portentous ~ signs of future trouble; an event that elicits
amazement or concern

portiere ~ a curtain in a doorway

portrait card ~ a photograph taken of a Civil War soldier

poseur ~ an imposter; an insincere person

potsy ~ a police officer, especially an overweight one

prattle, to ~ to babble; to talk aimlessly and pointlessly

presignify, to ~ to foreshadow; to foretell the future

priggish ~ behavior that is excessively formal and puritanical

prima facie ~ impressive, but incomplete, evidence

proleptic ~ addressing counterarguments before they are made

Psy Ops ~ CIA term for attempts to surreptitiously influence behavior and attitudes

pullulate, to ~ to grow prolifically; to swarm

pulped ~ to be reduced to a soft, soggy mess; to be trashed

punk ~ a lowlife; a thug; a tough person who causes trouble

purfled ~ heavily decorated, especially religious garments

pylon ~ a gate in ancient cities; warning cones on a road

quash, to ~ to put down; to crush; to defeat utterly; to quell

quench, to ~ to extinguish; to quell; to satisfy

querulous ~ a person given to frequent arguments and debates

quibble, to ~ to argue over minor points

quiddity ~ a minor detail in an argument; an insignificant detail

quip ~ a witty remark; a witty retort

quixotic ~ a person who is imaginative and unpredictable

quizzical ~ a curious attitude or person

quondam ~ a person who once occupied a role, but no longer does, like a former friend

R

raconteur ~ a witty person; a story teller

raddled ~ marked with rouge; a confused state; something that is twisted

raiment ~ clothing

raison d'etre ~ a reason for existence; the purpose something exists

rakehell ~ a libertine; a rowdy and randy man

rakish ~ provocative and mischievous behavior

rathe ~ an obsolete term for something that is premature

rattle brigade ~ slang term for the police force

raucous ~ loud and disorderly behavior

rawboned ~ a thin and angular physique; hidebound

reckon, to ~ to decide; to declare; to agree with (a Southern term)

rectitude ~ showing a moral and upright disposition

reek, to ~ to smell badly; to exude a foul substance

refugium ~ a restricted habitat in which organisms survive extinction

refulgent ~ shining brightly; a bright reflection

rejigger, to ~ to rearrange; to place objects in a different order relucent ~ a shiny or reflexive surface

renascent ~ returning to life; regaining influence

repine, to ~ to express dejection over what one does not have; to
  yearn

revenant ~ one who returns from the dead; one who returns after a
  long absence

rickhouse ~ a place where whiskey barrels are stored

-ridden ~ pestered by a type of person, such as priest-ridden or
  spouse-ridden

rime, rimy ~ a covering of frost; a crust

ringer ~ a lookalike; an imposter; a person who competes under
  false pretenses

riverine ~ alongside a river

rook, to ~ to cheat a person

rookie ~ an athlete in the first year of play; a person at a new job

root cellar ~ a place where vegetables are stored

rot, to ~ to suck; to stink; to do mean things

rotter ~ having a bad day or bad experience

rough-hewn ~ a person who lacks social graces; being in an
  unfinished state

roughish ~ having a rough surface, such as ocean water

roustabout ~ a handyman; a circus or carnival laborer

rover ~ a pirate; a privateer

rowhouse ~ a tenement; a rookery

rumpled ~ wrinkled; creased; disheveled; usually said of clothing

runes ~ letters in ancient German languages; objects used in telling
fortunes

runner ~ a messenger, especially in a financial district

russet ~ a brown or reddish-brown color

rustic ~ rural; a country setting

ruttish ~ to be in a state of sexual excitement; to be lustful

S

sailor ~ blue jacket, gob, jacktar, salt, shellback, tar

salacious ~ to speak or act in a vulgar or sexual manner

salt away, to ~ to save money or valuables for future use

saltless ~ insipid; lacking strength or vigor

sardonic ~ sarcastic in a humorous way; a statement that is bitter or
bittersweet

sate, to ~ to satisfy oneself fully with sensory pleasures

saturnine ~ moody or melancholy in disposition

saurian ~ like a reptile

savagerous ~ simultaneously savage and dangerous

scanties ~ bikini style underwear

scathe, to ~ to criticize harshly; to burn the skin

scoff, to ~ to eat quickly; to dismiss an idea or accomplishment as
unimportant

scoot, to ~ to run away quickly; to bolt

scraggy ~ disheveled; thin and sickly in appearance

scratch, to ~ to kill (Mafia term)

scrimmage, to ~ to be in a fight; to tussle

scrogglings ~ what is left in the field after the harvest (England term)

scrunch up, to ~ to fold up in fear; to crumple; to hunch up; to blanch

scry, to ~ to discern through occult means, such as with a crystal ball

scumble, to ~ to blur; to make bleary

scunner ~ a state of simultaneous fear and hate

scutch ~ peeled wood hanging on a branch; strips of bark

sedulously ~ a task performed with attention to detail; a task done diligently

seignior ~ a person of great importance; a feudal lord

sennet ~ a fanfare of trumpets

sententious ~ a moralizing statement delivered in a self-righteous manner

seraph ~ an angel of love

shallop ~ a small open boat used in shallow waters

sham ~ something that is not genuine, such as jewelry; counterfeit

shank, to ~ to miss the ball in football or golf; to stab a person with a short blade

shebang ~ the entire group, organization or operation; a hut (Civil War term)

shenanigan ~ a trick, often involving physical activity; playful
        misbehavior

shill ~ a person who, unknown to the audience, is part of the show;
        a fake

shimmer, to ~ to shine intermittently; to sparkle

showboat, to ~ to show off a skill, usually used in an athletic sense

shrimp ~ a small person

shrive, to ~ to grant forgiveness; to do penance; past tense is
        shrove, as in Shrove Tuesday

shuck, to ~ to strip; to husk; to pry open mollusks

shut-in ~ an invalid; a person who rarely leaves home

sickish ~ the condition of being sick; not appearing in good order

sidelong ~ alongside; at an oblique angle

sidewalk shed ~ used in construction sites to protect pedestrians
        from falling debris

sightless ~ something that is invisible

simoleon ~ slang for a dollar

sine qua non ~ an essential condition

sister, to ~ to join, such as one machine to another

skeletonize, to ~ to reduce to the bare bones

skin, to ~ to miss a kick in football; to scrape the skin in a fall; to peel or strip

skyey ~ celestial, ethereal, uranic

slabber, slobber ~ a drool or dribble; drivel

slab-sided ~ a thin or lanky person; a rawboned person

slacker ~ a lazy person; a person who shirks his or her duty

slander, to ~ to make false accusations about a person; to bear false witness

slangwhang, to ~ to use slang, often in a salacious manner

slather, to ~ to spread something thickly, such as jam or flattery

slavish ~ to act in a very obedient or subservient manner

slick ~ a disreputable person who possesses a lot of social skills; a swindler

slipstream ~ the turbulence behind a rapidly moving object, such as a plane

slithery ~ having a slippery nature; moving like a snake

sliver ~ a splinter of glass; a slender, usually sharp, object

slog, to ~ to work at a difficult task; to walk heavily or with difficulty

sluggard ~ a lazy person

slum, to ~ to live for free in another person's house

slumberous ~ a sleepy or drowsy state

slump, to ~ to slouch or fall over

sly rapper ~ a person who punches another person unexpectedly

smack-dab ~ to be in the middle of some task; exactly; correctly

small clothes ~ underwear

smattering ~ to possess a little knowledge; to be poorly informed

smear, to ~ to spread a substance onto something; to try to ruin a
　　　person's reputation

smell the coffee, to ~ to wake up; to face an unpleasant situation

smidgen ~ a small amount

smitten with ~ to be in love with a person; to be mightily
　　　impressed by something

smoking ~ an event or object that is thrilling

snaggle-toothed ~ to have irregularly shaped teeth

snake pit ~ a mental hospital; a psych ward in a hospital

snappish ~ peevish; rude; uncivil and uncouth; cantankerous

snip, to ~ to trim, such as hair or a lawn

snitch ~ an informant; a stoolie; a stool pigeon

snookered ~ hoodwinked; deceived; cheated

snuggery ~ a small room or apartment

soiree ~ a party

sorghum ~ a thick liquid such as molasses; syrup

sough ~ a soft sound like a mummer or rustle

spate ~ a sudden outburst of words; a large number of items
     suddenly appearing

spatter, to ~ to diffuse liquid in small drops; to cover a surface with
     drops

spiritualize, to ~ to make spiritual; to give a spiritual meaning to
     an event

splatter, to ~ to spatter; to splash

splendiferous ~ a wonderful event or scene; especially splendid

splenetic ~ to act in a hasty, excited manner; to act furiously

spoilsman ~ a recipient of political patronage or favors

sputter, to ~ to make a series of huffing sounds; to stutter

square accounts, to ~ to settle accounts

squawk, to ~ to complain loudly and frequently

squeegee ~ a street person who cleans windshields for a tip

squiggle, to ~ to wiggle one's fingers; to scribble; to doodle

squinch, to ~ to flinch; to crouch; to scrunch up; to squint

stash, to ~ to hide, usually money or valuables

steeple ~ a church tower; the spire is the top of the steeple

stem-winder ~ an excessively long or impressive speech

stint ~ to pass a period of time, usually in jail

strol-lop, to ~ to walk in long, fast strides

stumblebum ~ a clumsy person

surcease, to ~ to stop; to desist

susurrus ~ a soft rustling sound, such as the breeze makes; a
whisper

sutra ~ a teaching in the Hindu religion or in Buddhism

swain ~ a young man; a boyfriend

swan around, to ~ to dawdle; to walk without a destination; to
moon

swell ~ an affable person of wealth who enjoys partying
(Prohibition-era term)

T

taint, to ~ to corrupt morally; to become contaminated

tantalize, to ~ to beckon; to bedevil; to promise an outcome that can't be obtained

tar balls ~ tar deposits, such as on a beach

tatterdemalion ~ wearing tattered clothing; a decayed or broken structure

tatters ~ rags; shreds

tattersall ~ colored patches on a garment

tattle, to ~ to disclose a secret; to snitch; to squeal

tawny ~ a light brown color

tea ball ~ a tea bag

teetotaler ~ a person who abstains from drinking alcohol

ten-in-one ~ a carnival freakshow

tepid ~ lukewarm, like water or prose

teratogen ~ a substance that causes prenatal damage

terrene ~ earthly; of the earth

terse ~ speech or prose that is to the point; laconic

tetchy ~ irritable; peevish; cantankerous; an overly sensitive person thaumaturgic ~ pertaining to magic or to miracles

theeked ~ covered like thatch on a roof

thermophilous ~ organisms that prefer to live in heat

thievery ~ the action of thieves; the theft of a valuable item

thrall ~ to be emotionally attached to a person or an idea

threadbare ~ shabby clothing; tatters

throb, to ~ to beat or pulsate rhythmically

thump, to ~ to hit with great force; to land in a fall; to make a
thudding sound

thwart, to ~ to oppose an action of plan; to prevent something from
happening

tilth ~ cultivated soil

tine ~ the prong of a fork

tinkle ~ a light ringing or clinking noise

tint ~ a shade of color; tinct, tincture, tinge, trace

tipcart ~ a wagon that can be tipped; tumbril

tippler ~ a person who drinks a lot; an alcoholic

tiresome ~ something that is tedious to do; a task that wearies a
person

tittle ~ the dot above a "j" and "i"; a tiny dot on a paper

toasty ~ pleasantly warm, like a room or a car

toehold ~ a slight hold on something; a barely effective grip

toot ~ the sound of a horn; a binge of drinking

toplofty ~ haughty; egotistical; narcissistic

torpid ~ a state of weakness; lacking energy; torpor

torrid ~ blazing hot; an action filled with passion

touchy ~ easily aggrieved; tetchy; an unpredictable situation

toxoid ~ a weak form of a toxin

traduce, to ~ to make false statements to ruin a person's reputation; to slander

traipse, to ~ to walk eagerly or briskly

trammel, to ~ to impede; to prevent something from occurring

trash, to ~ to destroy; to insult or belittle a person or event

trawl, to ~ to dig up or collect fish and shellfish from the ocean floor

treenail ~ a nail that expands when inserted

tristful ~ a sad and melancholy state; a bittersweet feeling

troglodyte ~ a brutish person; an appearance-challenged person

trot, to ~ to run slowly; to proceed hastily to the toilet

truck with, to ~ to associate with

truculent ~ aggressive; ferocious; stormy

trudge, to ~ to walk slowly or heavily; to walk with much effort

tub-thumper ~ an adulator; a fan

tumbledown ~ a house in disrepair; a shanty

tumid ~ swollen; protruding

turbid ~ something that is opaque; something that is not clear

turgid ~ swollen; overly embellished prose or poetry

turn for ~ have a knack for doing something (Ozark)

tutmouthed ~ having thick lips or a prominent jaw (Old English)

tweedy ~ a nerd; a person who likes the outdoors

twiddle, to ~ to perform a frivolous task; to procrastinate

twinkle, to ~ to flicker; to sparkle or flash; to wink approvingly

two-fisted ~ a person given to fighting; a mean person

U / V

unbuttoned ~ bold; brazen; obvious

uncle ~ a person who is always watching (told to me in 1990 by a Macy's employee)

unguent ~ ointment; a salve

upper-shelf drinker ~ a person who prefers expensive alcohol

Ur- ~ a prefix meaning the original version or primitive version of a text

urbane ~ a sophisticate; a city dweller

ursine ~ like a bear

vacillate, to ~ to hesitate; to waver; to be indecisive

vagabond ~ a tramp; a vagrant; a person who has no fixed address

vagarious ~ capricious; unpredictable

Valhalla ~ the afterlife in German mythology

valiant ~ bold in the face of great odds; courageous; brave

Valkyrie ~ witches who decide who lives and dies in battles (German folklore)

valor ~ courage; endurance in adversity

vanilla ~ soft or easy, such as a task or a person; plain or bland in nature vapors ~ mysterious substances in the atmosphere that cause diseases; miasma

varmit ~ a rogue; a criminal; a lowlife

vascular ~ pertaining to the blood and to the heart

velvety ~ soft, smooth, satiny, slithery

venturesome ~ an audacious attitude; risk-taking behavior

verge ~ on the edge; a border; the end or limit of a place or an action

verminous ~ a filthy place that breeds disease; a place filled with vermin

verve ~ a state of activity or enthusiasm; a state filled with energy

vesper ~ pertaining to the evening

vet, to ~ to evaluate or inspect; to demonstrate as authentic

vex, to ~ to annoy or irritate; to prevent from fulfilling a task; to ambiguate

videosyncracies ~ favorite genres when watching television or DVDs

vindictive ~ a vengeful or spiteful attitude; purposely vengeful behavior

visage ~ one's face; one's overall appearance

viseme ~ specific movements of the lips in emitting sounds in lip reading vittles ~ foods (Southern term); victuals

vituperative ~ an angry outburst; to angrily berate someone

vixen ~ a high-strung and overly emotional woman

voluble ~ excitable; talkative; a bubbly and outgoing person

voluptuous ~ luxurious; beautiful in a fleshy, somewhat salacious
        manner

vouchsafe ~ to allow an event to occur; to respond approvingly

vulgarian ~ a rude, brutish person; a person who uses vulgarity
        routinely

vulpine ~ like a fox; having a sly or shrewd disposition

W

waddle, to ~ to walk with flat feet and a side-to-side motion

waders ~ boots

waggle, to ~ to move from side to side, to wiggle

wail, to ~ to cry aloud in grief or great emotion

wainscot ~ wood paneling in a room

wamble, to ~ to walk unsteadily; to feel ill

wampum ~ money (Native American)

wangle, to ~ to connive; to use trickery; to wiggle

war bonnet ~ a Native American headdress

warded ~ to shield from supernatural harm by the use of magical symbols

weed out, to ~ to remove from a group; to cull

welkin ~ the sky; the heavens

welsh, to ~ to refuse to pay one's debts; to cheat a person

wend, to ~ to travel; to wander; to easily make one's way

wetland ~ marshland; swamp; a mire

wheedle, to ~ to flatter; to treat favorably in order to get one's way

whipped ~ beaten; tired

whomp, to ~ to soundly defeat an enemy; to whop

whomp (whoop) it up for, to ~ to cheer; to rally; to applaud

whoop-de-do ~ an expression of mockery and minor disparagement

widdershins, withershins ~ the direction contrary to the sun; counterclockwise

will-o'-the-wisp ~ mysterious lights; a delusion

willy-nilly ~ a random or spontaneous event; uncontrollable events

wimp ~ a weak and timid man

wimpette ~ a female wimp

wince, to ~ to flinch; to express facial pain or discomfort

winding sheet ~ in olden days, a sheet in which to wrap a corpse

winger ~ a dancer; a hoofer

wink, to ~ to close one eye as a signal; to twinkle, to close or end (with "out")

winter ~ brumal; hibernal; hiemal

wiseacre ~ an arrogant know-it-all

witless ~ a dupe; a clueless person; an unintelligent person

wizened ~ shriveled and shrunken with age; wrinkled

wobble, to ~ to stagger; to roll sideways

wolfish ~ like a wolf; aggressive behavior

wont ~ habitual actions or inclinations

work, to ~ to manipulate a person or system in an unfair or
     nefarious way

worldling ~ a person with modern tastes; a person informed about
     world affairs

wrest, to ~ to extract by force

wriggle, to ~ to squirm; to wiggle; to extricate oneself from a
     precarious situation

writhe, to ~ to squirm or move in pain or great emotion

writhen ~ twisted or tormented

wuss, wusz ~ a person who hesitates to go along with the group

X / Y / Z

xenophobe ~ a person who is afraid of outsiders

yak, to ~ to talk incessantly; to yap

Yama ~ the Hindu god of death

yammer, to ~ to talk or complain incessantly

yaw, to ~ to deviate from a straight course; to move from side to
side

year-rounder ~ a person who lives in a shore resort, contrasted with
a day-tripper

yelp, to ~ to squeal; to whimper; to yowl

yestreen ~ yesterday evening

yoke-fellow ~ one's best friend; a chum

youngish ~ to have a youthful appearance; to look younger than
one's years

zeitgeist ~ the predominant intellectual orientation during a period
of time

zinger ~ an effective retort in an argument; a witty remark

zombification ~ the process of becoming a zombie

zonked ~ a state of extreme intoxication; knocked senseless

zoot suit ~ a 1920s style of dress with tight, tapered trousers and a
long jacket

My Favorite Color Words

Black

black and blue ~ having bruises on the skin; having welts

Black and Tan ~ the despised British police force in Ireland after
World War One

black art ~ black magic

black bag job ~ a covert operation conducted by a government
agency

black belt ~ an advanced degree in karate

black book ~ a date book; a book of phone numbers and addresses

black box ~ a device that records the activities of planes and trains

black death ~ bubonic plague

black diamond ~ coal

black dog ~ to be melancholy

black eye ~ a bruise to the eye socket

black face ~ stage makeup used by white people to resemble
African-Americans

black flag ~ a pirate's flag; the Jolly Roger

black gold ~ oil

black hand ~ the Mafia; organized crime influencing events

black hole ~ a collapsed star of immense gravity

black humor ~ sarcastic or off-color humor

black in the face ~ angry

black ink ~ to be in a profitable state in business

black light ~ light that is invisible to the naked eye

black list, to ~ to ostracize; to blackball

black magic ~ magic used for evil purposes, contrasted with white magic

Black Maria ~ a police paddy wagon

black mark ~ a mark given for bad behavior; a bad reputation

black market ~ illegal commerce

black mass ~ an obscene black magic ritual that parodies the Holy Mass

Black Monday ~ the day the stock market crashed

black money ~ a bribe

black ops ~ late twentieth century term for covert government operations

black out ~ to lose consciousness; a loss of electricity on a large scale

black pope ~ the head of the Jesuit order

black power ~ a 1960s political movement engaged in by radical African-Americans black sheep ~ a despised family member; the criminal in a family

Black Shirt ~ a fascist

black-tie affair ~ a formal dinner party

black top ~ the surface of a road

blackball, to ~ to ostracize; to prevent a person from joining an
organization

blackberry summer ~ Indian summer

Blue

blue ~ a state of sadness or depression

blue blood ~ to come from a rich or aristocratic heritage

blue book ~ a paper book used in essay exams in college

blue chip stock ~ a valuable stock likely to grow in value

blue collar laborer ~ laborers in factories, contrasted with white
collar office workers

blue devils ~ delirium tremens

blue-eyed boy ~ a favorite who can do no wrong

blue film ~ a pornographic movie

blue grass ~ country music played with fiddles and banjoes

blue in the face ~ exasperated; exceedingly annoyed

blue jacket ~ a sailor

blue laws ~ local laws that forbid openings of stores on Sundays

blue moon ~ two full moons in the same month; a long interval of
time

blue murder, to scream ~ to scream at the top of one's voice; to
complain aggressively

blue pencil, to ~ to edit or correct prose

blue print ~ schematic sketches or plans, usually in architecture

Blue Riband ~ the prize once given to the fastest Atlantic
        steamship

blue ribbon ~ a committee of experts and distinguished individuals

blue sky laws ~ accounting regulations in public stock offerings

blue streak ~ a streak of profanity, usually said in anger;
        interminable speech

blue, true ~ an honest person who would never deceive anyone; a
        loyal person

bluebeard ~ a husband who kills his spouse

bluecoat ~ a Union soldier in the Civil War

bluenose ~ a strict moralist; a puritanical person; a prig

blues, the ~ a style of music

blueshift ~ starlight that is approaching a viewer

bluesman ~ a performer of the blues

bluestocking ~ an intellectual woman; a pedantic professional
        woman

Brown

brown ~ a substance that is unrefined, like bread or sugar

brown bag it, to ~ to take a lunch from home to one's place of employment

Brown Bomber ~ Joe Louis, the heavyweight boxer and champion

brown nose, to ~ to flatter or fawn over a person

brown out ~ dimmed city lights

Brown Shirt ~ a Nazi storm trooper

brown study ~ melancholic contemplation of a topic

brownie ~ a junior girl scout; the chocolate pastry

brownie points ~ currying favor with a person by performing servile deeds

Gray

gray area ~ an area of uncertainty, especially involving morals

grayback ~ a Confederate soldier

graybeard ~ an old man

gray eminence ~ a person who possesses a secret influence on
        events

gray friar ~ a Franciscan

gray mail ~ blackmail

gray mare ~ an old person, usually a female

gray matter ~ the cell bodies of neurons in the brain

gray power ~ political influence wielded by senior citizens

gray propaganda ~ to publish bad news to keep worse news secret

Green

green ~ an inexperienced person; a person, usually young, who can be manipulated

Green Beret ~ a member of an elite special forces team

green card ~ what legal immigrants are granted

green cheese ~ what the moon is made of

green-eyed ~ jealous; gullible

green hand ~ an inexperienced person; an inexperienced sailor

green light ~ to receive permission to begin a project or journey

Green Party ~ an environmentally-oriented political party

green room ~ the room where a performer waits before going on stage

green, the ~ a golf course; a park

green thumb ~ a person who has a knack for growing plants

green, wearing the ~ identifying oneself as Irish, especially on March 17

greenbacks ~ money

greenhorn ~ an inexperienced person

greenhouse ~ a place where plants and vegetables are grown

greenhouse effect ~ a prior term for global warming and climate change

Pink / Purple

pink, pinko ~ a communist sympathizer; a fellow traveler

pink, to ~ to pierce; to cut the skin; to perforate

pink collar job ~ a job usually held by women

pink elephants ~ hallucinations experienced during delirium
        tremens

pink, in the ~ to be in good health; to be the best at something; to
        be well dressed

pink slip ~ notice that one's employment is terminated

purple, born to the ~ born a member of the aristocracy

Purple Heart ~ a medal for being wounded in combat

purple patch ~ flowery writing occurring within ordinary prose; a
        period of good luck

purple prose ~ a flowery style of writing

Red

red ~ a communist

red alert ~ imminent danger is about to happen

red badge ~ a bloodstain that demonstrates courage

red baiting ~ to accuse a person of being a communist

red-blooded ~ a born and bred American; a patriot; a true-blue
    American

red carpet treatment ~ to be treated as if royalty; to receive special
    treatment

Red Cross ~ a disaster relief organization

red dog, to ~ in football, the blitz of a linebacker; to charge the
    quarterback

red eye ~ an overnight trip on a plane or train; cheap whiskey

red flag ~ a symbol of battle; a symbol of danger

red-handed ~ to be caught committing a crime or infraction

red hat ~ a cardinal in the Roman Catholic church

red herring ~ a false lead in solving a crime

red herring prospectus ~ a preliminary prospectus given to
    potential stock buyers

red ink ~ to be in a state of debt in business

red letter day ~ a successful or victorious day; a memorable day

red light district ~ places in cities where vices, such as prostitution, are located

red menace ~ the communist threat to democracy

red nose ~ an alcoholic

red pencil, to ~ to edit, often in a critical manner

red shirt ~ an athlete who plays a fifth year in a college sport

red tape ~ bureaucratic rules and regulations

red tide ~ a bloom of algae in the ocean

redcap ~ a porter in railroad transportation

Redcoats ~ British soldiers in the Revolutionary War

redline, to ~ to discriminate, especially with respect to housing

redneck ~ a hick or rube; a Southern cracker; an uneducated working man

redshift ~ star light that is receding from a viewer

redskin ~ a derogatory name for a Native American

White

white ~ pure; hot

white beard ~ an old man

white collar crime ~ crime, usually nonviolent, in the financial
 sector

white collar worker ~ people who work in offices, contrasted with
 blue collar workers

white elephant ~ a valuable object too expensive to keep; an
 obvious and daunting fact

white face ~ stage makeup

white flag, to wave the ~ to surrender in a battle or in an athletic
 match

white glove treatment ~ to inspect carefully; to receive special
 treatment

white hope ~ a contender in boxing who is Caucasian

white hunter ~ a big game hunter

white knight ~ a person who comes to the rescue

white lady ~ a ghost; a specter whose appearance foretells death

white lie ~ to tell an inconsequential fib

white lightning ~ moonshine; rot gut

white line ~ the white markings on a road; a road

white-livered ~ a cowardly person; a cowardly deed

white magic ~ magic used for benevolent purposes, contrasted with
    black magic

white man's burden ~ the colonial subjugation and rule of
    indigenous peoples

white matter ~ the axons of neurons in the brain

white night ~ the midnight sun in the northern climes

white out ~ blinding snow; liquid paper used to cover mistakes in
    print

white pages ~ the pages in a telephone book listing individuals

white paper ~ an official government document on a topic

White Russians ~ Russians who fought the Bolsheviks during the
    Russian revolution

white supremacy ~ the belief that white people are superior to other
    races

white-tie ~ a formal party or dinner that exceeds the dress
    requirements of a black-tie party

white trash ~ members of the lumpen class; lowlives; the baseborn

white way ~ Broadway in Manhattan; the theater districts in cities

whitecaps ~ foamy waves

whitewash, to ~ to cover up or conceal crimes or misbehavior

Yellow

yellow ~ a coward

yellow alert ~ sounding an alarm that dangerous events may occur

yellow dog, to ~ to employ people on the condition they do not join an union

yellow flag ~ a flag that indicates the presence of disease on a ship

yellow journalism ~ sensational journalism not often connected to facts

yellow line ~ painted lines indicating lanes on a roadway

yellow pages ~ the pages in a phone book listing businesses

yellow peril ~ the threat that Asian people pose to Caucasians

yellow skin ~ jaundice

yellow streak ~ to show cowardice on a regular basis

My Favorite
Foreign Words

German

alte kampfer ~ old fighters; original members of the Nazi party

auf wiedersehen ~ good-by

blut ~ blood

blutkitt ~ bonds formed by shedding another person's blood

braten ~ roasted meat

dumbkopf ~ an ignorant, uninformed person

dunkle ~ dark

edel ~ precious; noble

festung ~ a fortress

gasthouse ~ an inn; a guest house

gegen ~ to be against something

geist ~ spirit; ghost

heimat ~ homeland; homesickness

henker ~ an executioner

herren ~ a title attached to a professional man

herrenvolk ~ the master race

kampf ~ a fight or battle; a struggle

kirsch ~ a cherry; brandy distilled from cherries

kitsch ~ art that is considered cheap and trashy and for the lumpen class

klatch ~ gossip exchanged in an impromptu group meeting

kreig ~ war

morgen ~ morning

nacht ~ night

putsch ~ an attempt, usually involving conspiracies, to overthrow a government

schadenfreude ~ taking delight in the suffering of other people

schatzi ~ a sweetheart

sieg heil ~ hail victory

stadt ~ a city

stalag ~ a prisoner of war camp

ubermensch ~ a superman, a superior man

untermensch ~ an inferior man, a worthless man

verboten ~ something that is forbidden

volk ~ the people

weiss ~ white

wunderbar ~ wonderful

Irish

amadan ~ literally, a moron

bad cess ~ bad luck often brought on by violating a superstition

banshee ~ a female specter whose appearance foretells death

bawn ~ an enclosure around a house; a yard; a fence or stone wall

blackthorn ~ a walking stick; a shillelagh

blarney ~ friendly speech meant to influence people; "throwing the bull"

bodach ~ a clown; a clowning person

boreen ~ a small road in the country

cead mile failte ~ a greeting—"A thousand welcomes"

clab ~ the mouth

codger ~ an old man

colcannon ~ mashed potatoes mixed with kale or cabbage

colleen ~ a young Irish woman or girl

craic ~ having fun; a party atmosphere

drop, a ~ a small amount of hard liquor

druth ~ an intellectually challenged person

-een ~ a suffix meaning small or tiny

feis ~ a festival, especially one involving music

for to ~ the word "for" is commonly placed before infinitives, e.g., "for to go"

futa fata ~ confused talk; nonsense

garda ~ the police force

get one's death, to ~ to die; the cause of a person's death

gift of gab ~ to talk smoothly and well; to master the art of blarney

gob ~ the mouth

gombeen man ~ a loan shark

good people, the ~ the fairies; the wee people who inhabit the other world

harvestmen ~ migrant farm laborers

himself / herself ~ how a person refers to another, often the spouse

leprechaun ~ a mischievous fairy said to possess a pot of gold; a shoemaker by profession

luck penny ~ a gift given by the seller to the buyer after a deal is struck

machree ~ a term of endearment meaning "my heart"

pattern ~ a religious ritual performed in certain places, such as at holy wells

pooka ~ an evil spirit; a poltergeist

poor mouth ~ poverty

poteen ~ homemade liquor; moonshine

prattie ~ a potato

scideen ~ a task easily done; small potatoes

shebeen ~ a low-class tavern; an unlicensed public house

shindig ~ a party with music and dancing

slainte ~ a toast while drinking, "To your health"

slean ~ a spade that cuts turf

stage Irishman ~ a person who acts Irish but does not possess the
            spirit

stirabout ~ milk and oatmeal porridge

Tinkers ~ Irish gypsies who roam the countryside; "Travelers" who
            have a bad reputation

wet ~ slang for a glass of beer, such as "Will you have a wet?"

Russian

apparatchik ~ a dutiful member of the Communist Party

Bolshevik ~ a communist; a follower of Lenin and Stalin

borscht ~ beet soup

boyar ~ a Russian aristocrat just below the level of royalty

dacha ~ a country house for wealthy and politically-connected
    families

dusha ~ the soul

Glasnost ~ Gorbachev's concept of political transparency

gulag ~ a prison, usually in Siberia, where political prisoners were
    sent

kasha ~ buckwheat

khleb ~ bread

kolkhoz ~ a collective farm

Komosol ~ the communist youth organization

kulak ~ a farmer, usually wealthy, who opposed collective farming

-nik ~ a suffix used by Americans to denote a stereotype, such as
    kolkhoznik

nomenklatura ~ the huge class of bureaucrats

Perestroika ~ Gorbachev's attempt to restructure the political system

pogrom ~ an organized persecution of a minority

Rodina ~ the Russian motherland

tovarich ~ a comrade

Stakhanovite ~ a highly efficient laborer; the original *Stakhanovite* was murdered by his fellow coworkers, who preferred not to work so diligently

voda ~ water

vodka ~ a clear alcoholic beverage from grains

Yiddish

bubela ~ a child; a grandchild; a friend; a term of endearment

bubkes ~ a small amount

chutzpah ~ an assertive or outlandishly bold deed or statement

cockamamy ~ not credible; a foolish scheme

dreck ~ garbage; dregs

fin ~ a five-dollar bill

futz around, to ~ to dwadle; to procrastinate

goy ~ a Gentile; a non-Jewish man

kibitz ~ idle talk; gossip

klutz ~ a clumsy or inept person

knish ~ square-shaped dough filled with potatoes or other
    vegetables

kosher ~ food or behavior that is religiously acceptable

kreplach ~ meat or cheese dumplings served in soup

kvetch, to ~ to complain

mazel tov ~ a toast "May you have good luck"

mensch ~ a man; a person; an honorable man

meshuggener ~ a crazy or confused person or situation

mishmash ~ a mixture that doesn't quite fit; a jumble; a medley

mitzvah ~ a small gift; a kind act

nebbish ~ a person who is difficult to please; a peevish person

nosh, to ~ to eat; to eat snacks

oy vey ~ an exclamation of surprise or exasperation

putz ~ a foolish person

schlemiel ~ a foolish person; an unlucky person

schlep, to ~ to walk in a slow or lazy manner; to go from one place
　　　　to another

schlock ~ standard items in retail; ordinary items

schlub ~ a nerd; a loser

schmaltz ~ sentimental behavior; sentimental art

schmear, to ~ a bribe or gratuity; to spread something on bread

schmooze, to ~ to be facile in conversation; to smooth talk

schmuck ~ a patsy; a person who was snookered; a disagreeable
　　　　person

schnozzle ~ the nose; a large nose

schtick ~ an act on stage; a performance regularly repeated

shekel ~ money

shiksa ~ a Gentile; a non-Jewish woman

zoftig ~ a good-looking, full-figured woman

My Favorite
Latin Phrases

ad majorem Dei gloriam ~ to the greater glory of God

alea jacta est ~ the die is cast

amor vincit omnia ~ love conquers all

ars longa, vita brevis ~ art is long, life is brief

carpe diem ~ seize the day; take the initiative

caveat emptor ~ let the buyer beware

caveat lector ~ let the reader beware

de profoundis ~ out of the depths; a statement of despair

dies irae ~ day of wrath; day of judgement

dulce et decorum est pro patria mori ~ it is sweet and pleasing to
die for one's country

eo ipso ~ by that fact; used in scholarly writing

et alia ~ and others, abbreviated et al.

exempli gratia ~ for example; abbreviated e.g.

ex libris ~ from the books of, a name on a bookplate

facilis descensus Averno ~ descending to hell is easy

Fata viam invenient ~ Fate will find a way

hic et ubique ~ here and everywhere

hic jacet ~ here lies, an expression found on tombstones

idem ~ the same as before; used in scholarly writing

id est ~ that is; abbreviated i.e.

in hoc signo vinces ~ by this sign (the Holy Cross) you will conquer

in saecula saeculorum ~ forever and ever

in vino veritas ~ in wine there is truth

locus in quo ~ the place in which; used in scholarly writing

mens sana in corpore sano ~ a sound mind in a sound body

morituri te salutamus ~ we who are about to die salute you, spoken by gladiators

nota bene ~ note well; used in scholarly writing

nunc et semper ~ now and always

ora pro nobis ~ pray for us

pax vobiscum ~ peace be with you

post hoc, ergo propter hoc ~ after this, therefore on account of this; a logical error

quid pro quo ~ favors given in expectation of return favors

quo vadis? ~ where are you going?

quod vide ~ which see; used in scholarly writing

requiescat in pace ~ rest in peace

semper fidelis ~ always faithful; motto of the U.S. Marine Corps *semper paratus* ~ always prepared; motto of the U.S. Coast Guard

sic semper tyrannis ~ thus ever to tyrants

sic transit gloria mundi ~ the glory of the world passes

siste viator ~ stop traveler; an expression on Roman tombstones

status quo ~ the existing state

sub rosa ~ an action done privately or in secret

sub specie aeternitatis ~ seen from an universal perspective

sursum corda ~ lift up your hearts

tempus fugit ~ time flies

urbi et orbi ~ to the city and the world; a message spoken by the
    pope

ut infra ~ as below; used in scholarly writing

ut supra ~ as above; used in scholarly writing

veni, vidi, vici ~ I came, I saw, I conquered; spoken by Julius
    Caesar

vincit omnia veritas ~ truth conquers all

My Favorite Body Words

ankles ~ hocks

breasts ~ boobs, bosom, bust, jugs, puppies, rack, tits, titties

buttocks ~ ass, behind, bum, bun, butt, caboose, can, derriere, duff
       fanny, hinny, hunches, hunkles, keister, rump, tuchus,
       tush

calves ~ shins, surals

eyes ~ peepers

face ~ kisser, mug, pan, puss

feet ~ dogs, hooves, pedals, puppies, tootsies

hands ~ grabs, mitts, paws

head ~ noggin, noodle, nut

heels ~ hocks

legs ~ gams, shanks, wheels

mouth ~ gob, maw

nose ~ beak, nozzle, schnoz, schnozzle; snout

ribs ~ slats

skin ~ hide

stomach ~ belly, craw

Verbs

to back off
to back up
to belly up
to bleed
to bloody
to bone
to breast
to cheek
to elbow
to eye
to eyeball
to face
to finger
to foot
to gum
to hand
to head
to jaw
to knee
to knuckle
to leg
to mouth
to muscle
to neck
to nose around
to palm
to rib
to skin
to teethe
to thumb
to toe
to tongue

My Favorite Beach Words

backrush ~ the movement of waves outward from the shore

backshore ~ the distance from the top of the high-water mark to the
      dune wall

barrel ~ the pocket of air under the curl of a large wave (surfer
      term)

beach face ~ the distance from the start of the low-water mark to
      the top of the high-water mark; foreshore

benthonic ~ the bottom of the sea

bight ~ an indentation in the shoreline; curvature of the shoreline

breaker zone ~ the place in the water where the waves are breaking

breakwater ~ a structure created parallel to the water to shield the
      shoreline; a seawall or bulkhead

comber ~ a large wave with a well-defined curvature

drink, the ~ the ocean; any substantial body of water

dune line ~ the edge of a beach; the highest point on a beach

dunes ~ rises of sand at the rear of beaches, having landward and
      seaward sides

estuary ~ the place at the mouth of a river where fresh water mixes
      with salt water

falling water ~ the flow of water away from the shore in a low tide;
      ebb tide

fetch ~ the distance a visible wave travels

flood tide ~ maximum reach of the high tide onto the shore

foreshore ~ the distance from the start of the low-water mark to the top of the high-water mark; beach face

headland ~ a cape; a promontory

jetty ~ a structure created perpendicular to the water to shield the shoreline or to direct the flow of the water; a groin

lagoon ~ a shallow body of water connected to, and partially shielded, from the sea

littoral ~ relating to the shoreline and the open sea

littoral zone ~ the zone of water from the beach to beyond the breaker zone

longshore currents ~ riptides; dangerous currents that run parallel to the shore

maverick ~ an exceptionally large wave (surfer term)

neap tide ~ the minimum change in water depth between the high and low tides

overwash ~ a storm surge

pelagic ~ living in the ocean; an event concerning the ocean

point break ~ the place where waves break on land that extends into the sea (surfer term)

promontory ~ rocks that project into the sea; a jetty

reach ~ the winding curves of a river

rills ~ ridges in sand formed by surf and wind; cusps

riparian ~ relating to the shoreline and to tidal water

riprap ~ boulders placed in the water to slow the waves and prevent
    beach erosion

rising water ~ the flow of water toward the shore in a high tide;
    flood tide

sandbar ~ a buildup of sand that makes deep water shallow; a shoal

scarp ~ vertical edges of a beach or marshland created by tides

shore drift ~ the continuous change in the shoreline owing to waves
    and wind

spit ~ a narrow projection of beach or marshland into the sea

spring tide ~ the maximum change in water depth between high
    and low tides

spume ~ foam given off waves in windy conditions; spindrift

swash ~ agitated movement of waves; water between a sandbar and
    the shore

uprush ~ the movement of waves inward toward the shore

waterline ~ the surface of the sea

wrack ~ the collection of seaweed and debris at the water's edge

My Favorite Nautical Words

abaft ~ proceeding toward the stern (rear of the vessel)

adrift ~ a vessel in motion but not under the control of the crew

afore ~ proceeding toward the bow (the front of the vessel)

all hands ~ an event involving all persons on board a vessel

anchor lights ~ white lights indicating a vessel is at anchor

astern ~ proceeding toward the stern (rear of the vessel)

ballast ~ heavy objects placed in the hold to stabilize a vessel

bar pilot ~ a pilot brought on board to steer a vessel into a harbor

beam ~ the width of a vessel at its widest

beat to quarters ~ prepare for battle; man battle stations

beyond the ken ~ beyond the horizon; objects that are too distant
           to see

bilge ~ filthy water that must be pumped out of the bottom of a
       vessel

bitt ~ a heavy rotund pole around which a vessel's lines are
      moored; a bollard

burdened vessel ~ the vessel that must give way to avoid a collision

camber ~ the curvative of the vessel from the center outward

capstan ~ a machine used to haul the anchor in and out of the water

coaming ~ the raised portion of a hatch above the deck

cut of the jib ~ the shape and color of a sail, identifying the
                nationality of a vessel

derelict ~ an abandoned vessel

devil seam ~ to be between the devil and the deep blue sea

draft ~ the depth of the hull below the waterline when the vessel is
        fully loaded

fathom ~ a six-foot unit of measurement below the waterline

fitting out ~ the period in which a new vessel is tested on the open
        sea; a sea trial

float ~ a barge hauled by a tug; used to carry trains and cargo

flotsam ~ wreckage of a vessel; jetsam is cargo thrown off a vessel

following sea ~ waves proceeding in the same direction as the
        vessel

footloose ~ sails flapping in the wind; a vessel able to sail in any
        direction

foul ~ to be entangled; to be dirty or encrusted

founder, to ~ to fill with water and sink

grog ~ rum; liquor

gunnel, gunwale ~ a railing on the upper deck of a vessel

hatch ~ opening in a deck through which cargo is loaded and
        unloaded

head ~ the most forward part of a vessel; a toilet

heave, to ~ the up and down motion of a vessel; to pitch

hold ~ the interior of a vessel where cargo is stored

keel ~ the main portion of the hull of a vessel

ladder ~ what stairs are called on a vessel

launch ~ a small boat launched from a larger boat

league ~ an approximate distance of 2.5 nautical miles

lee side ~ the side of a ship protected from the wind

leeward ~ facing the same direction in which the wind is blowing

lighter ~ a small vessel that travels between the shore and large
vessels; a tender

line ~ what a rope is called on a ship

list, to ~ to lean or tilt to one side; to heel; to roll

moor, to ~ to attach a vessel's lines to a bollard; to dock

mothball fleet ~ vessels no longer in use, but which are not scraped

nautical mile ~ a distance of 6,080 feet (American)

oilskin ~ foul-weather gear

pitch, to ~ to heave; the up and down movement of a vessel

pitchpole, to ~ to capsize with the stern going over the bow; to go
upside down

poop deck ~ the rear of a vessel; the fantail

port side ~ the left side of a vessel facing forward; illuminated by a red light

privileged vessel ~ the vessel that has the right of way

prow ~ the bow, the front or forward side of a vessel

reeve, to ~ to thread lines through blocks or pulleys

roll, to ~ the side to side motion of a vessel; to list

run aground, to ~ to get stuck in shallow water

scrap, to ~ to demolish a vessel no longer in use for metal and parts

scuppers ~ openings along railings to allow water to drain off decks

scuttle, to ~ to deliberately sink a vessel

seakeeping ~ a vessel that can sail in storms

sheer ~ the bow to stern curvature of a vessel

slip ~ the place between piers where vessels dock

slush fund ~ leftover oil and grease once sold by ships' cooks for profit

snag ~ an object on or below the waterline that can damage a vessel

starboard ~ the right side of a vessel facing forward; illuminated by a green light

stern ~ the rear half of a vessel; aft

stowage ~ the amount of space on a vessel available for cargo and
    supplies

strike the colors, to ~ to surrender in a sea battle

tack, to ~ to sail in zigzag directions when going into the wind

tender ~ a lighter

touch and go, to ~ to touch the bottom of the sea, but not to run
    aground

tramp steamer ~ a cargo vessel that does not have fixed ports of
    call

vanishing point ~ the point at which a vessel will tip and capsize

wake ~ the turbulence behind a vessel

weather side ~ the side of a vessel experiencing weather and wind

weigh anchor, to ~ to bring up the anchor

windward ~ facing the direction the wind is coming from; looking
    into the wind

yaw ~ the side to side swaying motion of a vessel

My Favorite Baseball Words

ace ~ the main starting pitcher

ball ~ pellet, pill, pit

ballpark ~ band box, orchard, pasture, pea patch

barber ~ a pitcher who shaves the edges of the plate, throwing near
the batter

barnstorming ~ minor league teams that travel frequently

base ~ bag, sack

basket catch ~ to catch the ball with both hands against the chest

bat ~ lumber, stick, timber, wood

battery ~ the pitcher and catcher considered as an unit

bean ball ~ a pitch aimed at the batter's head

beat out, to ~ to arrive safe on base a moment before the ball
arrives

benched ~ to be removed from the starting team

bench jockey ~ a player on the bench who belittles opponents

benchwarmer ~ a player who rarely plays

bleachers ~ the stands; cheap seats in the outfield

bonehead play ~ a foolish mistake that shouldn't have been made

boot, to ~ to make an error on a ground ball

box score ~ the newspaper summary of a game listing statistics brushback ~ a pitch deliberately thrown near the batter

bullpen ~ the place where relief pitchers warm up

bush leagues ~ the minor leagues

carpet ~ the outfield grass

caught looking ~ a batter who didn't swing at the third strike

cellar ~ last place in the league standings

chin music ~ a pitch that nearly hits the batter in the head

choke, to ~ to fail to make an important play at a crucial moment

circus catch ~ to make an acrobatic catch

cleanup hitter ~ the fourth batter in the lineup, usually a home run
        hitter

clothesline catch ~ a low line drive that is caught just before the
        ball hits the ground

collar ~ to play an entire game without getting a hit

college try ~ to perform as well as one can against a superior team

curve ball ~ a pitch that breaks away from the batter

designated hitter ~ a batter who is in the game but does not play a
        position on the field

diamond ~ the infield

doubleheader ~ two games on the same day; a twin bill

double play ~ to get two outs on a single play

fast pitch ~ heat, hummer, mustard, smoke

fireman ~ the ace relief pitcher on a team

folly floater ~ a soft pitch lobbed toward the plate

foul tip ~ a foul ball that goes backward over the catcher

free agent ~ a player who changes teams to make more money

gap ~ the wide spaces between outfielders; power alleys

glove ~ mitt, the leather

go down swinging, to ~ to strike out by swinging and missing the
ball

go to bat for, to ~ a substitute hitter

goat ~ the player who causes a game to be lost

grandstand, to ~ to show off; to hot dog

grapefruit league ~ winter leagues in the South; the stove league

grass cutter ~ a sharply hit ground ball

green light ~ a runner who has permission to steal a base

handcuffed ~ to be unable to catch a ground ball that takes a
bad hop

hitless wonder ~ a very poor hitter

hook ~ to remove a pitcher from the game

hot corner ~ third base

in the hole ~ a ball hit in the gap between outfielders

journeyman ~ a player frequently traded

knuckleball ~ a slowly thrown pitch with erratic movement

Ladies Day ~ a game in which ladies were admitted at lower prices

laugher ~ a one-sided game in which a team wins decisively

leg it out, to ~ to run at full speed despite being a certain out

line drive ~ a very hard hit ball at head level

load up, to ~ to coat the ball with a foreign substance, such as
saliva

long reliever ~ a relief pitcher who pitches a large number of
innings

meal ticket ~ the most important and talented player on a team

mound ~ the pitching mound, 10 inches high and 60 ft., 6 inches
from home plate

nail the runner, to ~ to capture a base runner in an out, usually
after a long throw

night cap ~ the second game of a doubleheader

off the table ~ a pitch that drops steeply as it approaches home plate on the block ~ a player offered in a trade

one-bagger ~ a base hit

opener ~ the first game in a doubleheader

passed ball ~ an error by the catcher

phenom ~ a talented player

pick off, to ~ the pitcher unexpectedly nailing a careless opponent
    at first base

pinch hit, to ~ one batter substituting for another

pull the string, to ~ to unexpectedly throw a slow pitch after a
    series of fast pitches

rain check ~ what fans get when the game is called on account of
    rain

rhubarb ~ a fight on the field (coined by Red Barber)

ride, to ~ to belittle opposing players; to belittle a poorly
    performing teammate

sacrifice, to ~ to purposely make out so a runner can advance a
    base

scorecard ~ list of starting players in a game with room to record
    their statistics

scratched ~ removed from the line up at the last minute

scroogie ~ a screwball

sent to the clubhouse ~ thrown out of the game; sent to the showers

seventh inning stretch ~ when fans stand and stretch

shag flies, to ~ to catch fly balls, usually in practice

shoestring catch ~ to catch a ball just before it hits the ground; a
clothesline catch

short reliever ~ a relief pitcher who faces only a few batters

sit in the cat bird seat, to ~ to be in a winning position (coined by
Red Barber)

slider ~ a pitch that breaks sharply over the plate; thrown with more
speed than a curve ball

slugger ~ a home run hitter

spitball ~ a pitch covered with saliva or a foreign substance

squeeze play ~ to attempt to bunt while the runner on third base
charges home plate

steal, to ~ to successfully advance by running from one base to
another

stopper ~ the ace relief pitcher

sweet spot ~ a ball pitched in the zone a batter likes

tag, to ~ to physically make an out by touching a runner

tag one, to ~ to hit a long home run

tape measure ~ a very long home run

Texas Leaguer ~ a soft base hit that lands between the infield and
the outfield

triple play ~ to make three outs in the same play

wheelhouse ~ the part of home plate favored by a batter

Words that Are Frequently Confused

abjure, to ~ to abstain from voting or participating
adjure, to ~ to command or appeal

abstruse ~ a topic that is very difficult to understand
obtuse ~ a person who is limited in understanding

adverse ~ unfavorable conditions
averse ~ to be in opposition to a person or situation

aid, to ~ to give help; to assist
aide ~ a person who gives help or assists

all ready ~ a person is prepared
already ~ a situation or event has been completed and is now past

ambiguous ~ the meaning of a phrase or of an event is not clear
ambivalent ~ a person holds two attitudes regarding an action

anybody ~ is one word, unless a particular body is indicated
anyone ~ is one word, unless a particular person is indicated
anything ~ is one word, unless a particular thing is indicated
anyway ~ is one word, unless a particular way is indicated
any time ~ is always two words regardless of the time

assure, to ~ to declare that something is true or correct
ensure, to ~ to make sure something happens

below ~ to be under a person or object; to be in an inferior position
beneath ~ to be directly underneath a surface or object

beside ~ next to; objects that are contiguous
besides ~ in addition to

biannual ~ indicates an event that occurs twice a year
biennial ~ indicated an event that occurs every two years

can ~ is to do what is possible
may ~ is to do what one is allowed to do

classic ~ an ideal, a model
classical ~ refers to Ancient Greece or Rome

climatic ~ weather conditions
climactic ~ the dramatic highlight of a movie or book

complacent ~ is to be smug and self-satisfied in attitude
complaisant ~ is to be cooperative and agreeable

compose, to ~ to write or create something
comprise, to ~ to consist of components

contagious diseases ~ are spread by contact with a person
infectious diseases ~ are spread by contact with the environment
(air, water)

continually ~ an event that repeats at regular intervals
continuously ~ an event that occurs nonstop

convince, to ~ to get people to share a particular opinion or viewpoint
persuade, to ~ to get people to act in certain ways

crumble, to ~ to break into pieces, such as a cookie
crumple, to ~ to bend; to fold up; to scrunch

deprecate, to ~ to disparage and belittle
depreciate, to ~ to reduce in value; to lower the price of an object

discomfit, to ~ to harass; to prevent the occurrence of an action
discomfort, to ~ to make uncomfortable

discreet ~ something that is kept quiet; a sensitive broaching of a
topic

discrete ~ separate items or events; unrelated items or events

farther ~ physical distance
further ~ a non-physical distance; new items are added to what is
    already present

flare ~ a light; a fire
flair ~ a talent or gift for doing something; a knack for doing
    something

flounder, to ~ to have difficulty in succeeding or in walking
founder, to ~ to fill with water and sink

gleam ~ a brief, but intense light; a reflection of light
glean ~ to sift; to cull; to gather information

glint, to ~ to sparkle; to flash
glisten, to ~ to shine; to reflect light

historic ~ an important event, like an assassination or a battle
historical ~ something based on history, such as a theory or a novel

if I was ~ being in a possible situation
if I were ~ being in an impossible situation or a purely theoretical
    situation

imbrue, to ~ to stain
imbrute, to ~ to descend to the level of brutes and thugs
imbue, to ~ to permeate; to diffuse

into ~ to enter a particular place or situation
in to ~ all other uses of the term beyond the one indicated above

lessen ~ to reduce in number or severity
lesson ~ information that is taught, such as psychology

let's ~ contraction for "let us"
lets ~ allows, permits certain actions

loath, to ~ to be unwilling to cooperate
loathe, to ~ to hate or dislike

luxuriant ~ profuse growth, such as hair or grass; lush
luxurious ~ sumptuous and expensive, such as an apartment

malfeasance ~ illegal acts by elected officials or authority figures
misfeasance ~ a crime or misbehavior

mantel ~ a shelf attached to a wall or fireplace
mantle ~ a garment that covers a person; a cloak

material ~ physical matter
materiel ~ supplies, usually for an army

may be ~ a conditional state; something that may happen
maybe ~ perhaps

militate, to ~ to have a particular effect that works against something
mitigate, to ~ to reduce the effect of something; to assuage

nauseous ~ what causes nausea, such as fumes or food poisoning
nauseated ~ what one feels when experiencing nauseous situations

paean ~ an artistic expression of praise for a person, usually in a
    poem
peon ~ a peasant; an unimportant person

perspicacious ~ shrewdness; insight; sound judgment
perspicuous ~ clear writing or speaking

practical ~ easily accomplished; applied, not theoretical
practicable ~ something that can be done or put into effect

prone ~ to lie face down
prostrate ~ to be prone because of exhaustion or submission
supine ~ to lie face up

repellant ~ something that drives a person away
repugnant ~ something that elicits dislike or disgust in a moral sense
repulsive ~ something that elicits a visceral dislike and withdrawal
revulsion ~ something that elicits a visceral dislike or disgust

restive ~ nervous; fidgety
restful ~ calm; content; refreshed

scrumptious ~ something that is delightful, usually used in reference
        to food
sumptuous ~ something that is extravagant or expensive

sensual ~ appealing to the senses; expressing sexuality
sensuous ~ appealing to the senses or to sexuality in an artistic way

sometime ~ a period of indefinite length
some time ~ a period of definite length

stationary ~ not moving; being immobile
stationery ~ writing paper and supplies

tousle ~ rumpled hair
tussle ~ a fight; a struggle

torpid ~ dull; unresponsive
turbid ~ impossible to see through or understand
turgid ~ swollen; a verbose and bombastic style of speech or writing
turpitude ~ being in a depraved state; acting immorally

tortuous ~ winding and circuitous, such as a path; crooked; mazy
torturous ~ causing pain or torture

valance ~ drapery hung below a mattress at the edge of a bed
valence ~ a chemical term for the attraction between elements

venal ~ a person who can be corrupted; an immoral or illegal act
venial ~ a minor sin; contrasted with mortal sin

who's ~ who is
whose ~ of whom; who owns an item; who possesses an item

will ~ something that will actually exist in the future
would ~ something that may or may not exist in the future

Words that are Often Unnecessary

The words below in *italics* are often unnecessary.

admit *to* a mistake

advance planning

a *little* baby

a *new* baby

blurt *out*

check *out*

climb *up*

end result

fall *down*

flanked *on both sides*

free gift

free sample

future plans

join *together*

link *together*

local residents

minute details

most basic

opening gambit

over-and-over *again*

past achievements

past experiences

plan *ahead*

razed *to the ground*

reason is *because*

reason *why*

recite *out loud*

regression *back*

reiterate *again*

repeat *again*

careful, close scrutiny

so as to

surrounded *completely*

temporary respite

thought *to himself or herself*

total annihilation

totally destroyed

true facts

up following to buoy, to lift, to loosen

usual procedures

vast majority

very next one

weather *conditions*

Fancy Words
to Avoid

Although they are distinguished, it is better to avoid using the words on the left. They should be used only in scholarly writing, but maybe not even in scholarly writing.

afflatus ~ inspiration; creativity inspired by a god
agonistic ~ aggressively argumentative
albescent ~ pale; white
anamnesis ~ recollections (a term mostly used in psychotherapy)
autochthonous ~ indigenous; native to a place, such as a plant or
                animal
balneal ~ bathing, bathroom
borborygmus ~ rumblings of the stomach
cacography ~ misspellings; illegible handwriting
cicerone ~ a guide or mentor
collyrium ~ eyewash
decussate ~ an intersection; something that is intersected
demarche ~ a maneuver, usually made by armies
depilate, to ~ to remove bodily hair
discommode, to ~ to disturb
divagate, to ~ to digress, as in a speech
doppelganger ~ a look-alike, usually in a supernatural context
effluvium ~ a bad odor; a vapor
eristic ~ argumentative
eruct, to ~ to belch
evaginate, to ~ to turn inside out
gasconade ~ boasting; bragging
glabrous ~ bald; smooth, such as a stone
hermeneutic ~ interpretation of a story, usually Biblical
ichthyoid ~ fish-like
ignescent ~ flammable; giving off sparks
jejune ~ something that is dull or boring
jeremiad ~ a lamentation; predictions of impending doom
lachrymose ~ a state of sadness and grief
lenitive ~ something that soothes or softens
longueur ~ a state of boredom; boring prose

masticate, to ~ to chew
mephitic ~ malodorous; putrid; rancid
minatory ~ something that is dangerous; something that threatens
munificence ~ extreme generosity
myrmidon ~ a criminal; a thug; a lackey
orgulous ~ an excessively proud person
orotund ~ a pompous, self-important person
otiose ~ indolent; lazy; having no function
quidnunc ~ a person who engages in gossip
rubescent ~ blushing
rufescent ~ reddish in color or complexion
rugose ~ wrinkled; crinkled
salubrious ~ healthy; leading to good health
scabrous ~ indecent acts or speech; salacious
simulacrum ~ a semblance or resemblance of people or objects
tenebrous ~ dark; obscure
tergiversate, to ~ to equivocate; to hesitate
termagant ~ an annoying, usually elderly, woman
velleity ~ a wish that is never achieved

Printed in the United States
By Bookmasters